£ 2.00 (BA)

The Devil's Shake

Along the borderlands Joe Pilgrim had become a legend in his own time. Now that he has taken up ranching, though, he doesn't aim to wear a badge any more. Even so, he's talked into taking the honorary position of marshal by the friendly folk of Willow Flats.

Then, shockingly, this peaceful town erupts into violence, fire and murder with the arrival of a bunch of suspicious characters. First there is the scheming gambler LaVere, the genial Big Ade and the viperish little Jollo. Then there are a pair of wild young owlhooters and a mysterious sniper who takes potshots at lone riders. The territory is menaced, as is the Pilgrim Ranch and the marshal's beautiful new wife, Arabella.

Once again, Joe Pilgrim must take up his guns until, in a final pageant of hot lead and grim death, peace is finally restored to Willow Flats.

The Devil's Shake

JAY HILL POTTER

A Black Horse Western

ROBERT HALE · LONDON

© Jay Hill Potter 2001
First published in Great Britain 2001

ISBN 0 7090 6997 9

Robert Hale Limited
Clerkenwell House
Clerkenwell Green
London EC1R 0HT

Typeset by
Derek Doyle & Associates, Liverpool.
Printed and bound in Great Britain by
Antony Rowe Limited, Wiltshire.

For Joycie, a Pilgrim fan from way back.
And for Kelly-Anne, Karen and Alan – and John.

Part One
Lawman's Way

ONE

Pilgrim saw the blow coming, twisted a bit, leaned his head to one side. Cooley's fist grazed his neck, not shaking him. And already he was moving again, sinking his knuckles into Cooley's belly just above the ornate belt-buckle.

Cooley went 'Oof' and bent double. Instinctively, though, he reached for his gun. But he wasn't what you might call mighty fast; and Pilgrim was.

'Let it go, Ed,' he said. 'I don't want to shoot you. But I would.'

His gun was already pointed at Cooley's face. He reached with his other hand, lifted Cooley's weapon. Cooley put a hand across his punished middle, hugged it, his knees bending. Then he was half-crouching.

And Pilgrim said, 'Stay like that, Ed. Except for your left hand. Reach that around you an' get that sticker outa the back o' your belt. Do it very gently.

That blade's caused too much misery already. Trake's dead. But I guess you know that already, don't you?'

'I didn't know. I swear. . .'

'Drop the knife,' Pilgrim cut in. Cooley did this and straightened up, backed. His eyes when he looked straight from an unshaven face at the other man were almost beseeching.

'I aimed at his arm, Joe. I just wanted to stop him. He insulted Carrie, an' he drew his gun an' threatened to pistol-whip me. I'm no gunny, Joe, you know that.'

'I do. With a gun I've always been faster'n you. . . .'

'You're the fastest I've ever known, *amigo*. I allus said. . . .'

Pilgrim interrupted again, sounding almost as if he were spitting in disgust. 'And you were the fastest I've ever seen with a blade. Particularly in the throw. Hell, I've seen you pin a bug to a chunk o' timber. You got Trake plumb in the middle of the back before he hit the batwings. He was dead when he hit the boardwalk, and – damn you, Ed – you were outa the back door by then.'

'You're taking me back, Joe?' It was a question rather than a statement.

'I'm taking you back,' Pilgrim echoed. 'Hell, I'm the town marshal. What did you expect when you got off your horse and waited for me?'

Cooley didn't answer the question properly, said, 'I didn't figure Trake was hurt bad. I just figured I'd light outa town for a while.'

'An' left Carrie standing there! She's with my Arabella now an' things ain't pretty with them, Bella's man after her best friend's man, murderin' skunk that he turned out to be. Mount up, Ed, the talkin's over.'

They both went back to their saddles. Pilgrim told Cooley to ride a little ahead of him, and this the man did. He was lean, tow-headed, kind of handsome. Right now he looked disconsolate. But Pilgrim couldn't pity him.

Pilgrim remembered the dead Trake and Trake's grieving girl, Carrie. And, remembering other things, he said:

'I figured you'd have another knife. You had to run home to get your hoss. You'd pick up a knife there, wouldn't you – I figured that? You always had a collection. Fancy! Did you see your ma?'

He had been sort of talking things through. He only spoke louder on the last question, and Cooley answered that.

'She was out.'

'If she was in town she'd soon find out what happened,' Pilgrim said.

They did not talk after that. Night came. Clear skies speckled with stars. There was a small breeze. Weather had been good lately, not too hot

11

here in this territory where, oftimes, the sun could sear and blister unprotected human flesh.

They saw the lights of town and Cooley slowed his horse, though not speaking at first. But then he suddenly said, 'I'm gonna take off. You wouldn't shoot me in the back.'

'Try me,' Pilgrim said.

'We used to be such good friends.'

'That was a long time ago, back home when we were kids. Long before either of us came to this place.'

'I've got to try. I. . .'

'Try then. I'll put a pill in your shoulder, I swear.'

Joe always meant what he said, Cooley knew that. He wouldn't miss either. And when Joe said, 'Move on! Or I'll ride you into town with cuffs on,' Cooley did as he was told. And neither of them spoke again.

TWO

The town was called Willow Flats, obviously because it had a creek nearby it on the banks of which willows grew profusely, threatening from time to time to take over the territories nearest to them, necessitating a 'clean-up' now and then. Trails were cut on each side of the creek, three in all, leading to that side of town. Cooley and Pilgrim took the widest of these. It led into the main street and was hard-baked and clear.

The territory was flat and well grassed, good range on which cattle grazed at will. There was no big greedy ranch thereabouts but plenty of small and medium-sized spreads which gave the town its business. It was not a large outpost but compact, becoming somewhat cluttered now. Buildings were growing like tumbleweed on the side where there was no creek and no willows.

In the main, the place was becoming mighty

prosperous. Law-abiding too, mainly due to its marshal, Joe Pilgrim. He'd been the lawman for some time except for minor snags. . . . Until the terrible Cooley/Trake business came about.

Heads turned in the night under the bright lights – and the marshal and his captive were riding side by side now.

A lean youth walked out into the middle of the main drag, pointed a finger at Ed Cooley and shouted, 'I want him!'

'Move out of the way, Lenny,' said Pilgrim. 'This man's my prisoner now an' the law will do its business.'

The two riders had halted. Ed Cooley's face was drawn, no longer handsome, his eyes wide. The youth who confronted him was Lafe Trake's brother who was not pointing any more, had his hands at his belt.

Feet shuffled. Faces stared. But there were no more voices till Pilgrim spoke, almost softly, but clearly.

'Don't push me, Lenny. Not me. Move aside.'

A girl came out of the crowd. She said, 'Come on, Lenny. This will do no good to anybody.'

'Leave me be, Carrie,' Lenny said.

But then there was another girl.

They were a mighty attractive pair. The second one, with dark-gold hair, green-eyed, was the marshal's wife, Arabella, 'Bella' to her friends, and the dark-haired pretty one next to her was one of the best of those.

'Come with us, Lenny,' Bella said. 'You know that Joe will do what he has to do.'

Lenny took his hands away from his belt, lowered his head, turned and followed the two young women.

Marshal and prisoner went on towards the stout adobe jailhouse, out front of which Pilgrim's two deputies stood: they'd been ready to step forward if needs be. But townsfolk were going about their business now.

Cooley was led through the office to the cell-block and locked up. The older of the two deputies, known as Pug because that was what he'd once been, slept in a bunk next to the kitchen. Pilgrim had a small, neat house on the back end of town. The second deputy had a regular billet in a neighbouring hotel. His name was Jakeson, so everybody called him Jake, though his first name was really William.

Pilgrim left the jail in the capable hands of the two men. He didn't aim to be away long. There was only one man in the cells. But there'd be bad feeling against that man and the marshal figured there might be some misguided individuals who reckoned they should do something.

Pilgrim mounted his horse and aimed him homewards, which wasn't far. But they both needed washing, and rest and sustenance.

There was a small stable outside the house on the edge of town which Pilgrim had purchased from a widow-lady who wanted to join her daughter and husband and kids back East. Since settling in this territory the neat, smallish place was his second buy of that kind he'd made since he hit this territory. He also had a small ranch way out of town, past the smallish spread which had been run for many years by his wife Arabella's father, Pete Teller. Arabella, an only child, barely remembered her mother who had died young: the far West had been a tough place for female folk in those very early days.

Pilgrim had met Arabella during the time when he was helping her father, Pete, avert a range war.[1]

Pilgrim had been brought up on a ranch which was being run by his father, still known then as 'Marshal Joe', back on the Pecos. The old ex-lawman was helped enormously by young Joe's sister, Rebbie, and her husband Cal.

As a troubleshooter Joe had done a lot of fiddle-footing, found it hard to settle down to mundane, if hardworking ranch life. He remembered too that his father had been way past his, young Joe's, age when he quit the trail and the badge-toting and took to ranching.

---

[1] See 'The Last Go-Down'.

But with young Joe, something happened: the marshal of Willow Flats died suddenly from a fever and the younger man, son-in-law of the popular Pete Teller, was offered the job.

Young Joe had toted a badge before, if only briefly, and both his wife and his father-in-law (kindly and understanding people) had recommended he take the job.

The Pilgrim Ranch, not yet given a name, fancy or otherwise, was now run by a middle-aged, childless couple, the Cardozas, who knew their business well, with old Pete keeping an eye on them and Arabella and Joe visiting as often as possible.

Things had gone pretty smoothly. The well-known Pilgrim professionalism with a shooting iron – particularly here in the borderlands – was good for the peace of Willow Flats and nothing very terrible had happened there till the Cooley and Trake trouble.

And, making for home, Pilgrim was not sure what he was getting into now.

He stabled his horse, entered the house through the kitchen, heard the two women talking but no male voice. He was glad that dark Carrie had stayed. She was somebody he badly needed to talk to.

He shouted, 'I'll wash up first,' heard his wife's sweet voice in reply.

Quickly, he entered the cosy sitting-room; the

two girls were there, nobody else. And Arabella said, 'Lenny went, said he didn't want to see you again yet awhile.'

'That figures,' Pilgrim said.

His wife went on quickly, 'Carrie has been telling me things. I said I'd pass them on to you, but she has insisted that she tell them to you herself. So I'll go make more coffee. I've also baked some of those currant-and-pecan cakes you like so much.'

Without further comment the slim girl with the dark-gold hair left the other girl and the man alone together.

Pilgrim looked at Carrie, saw that there were tears in her dark eyes.

Her voice was thick and shaky when she broke out with, 'I feel I'm partly to blame, Joe, for what happened – between Ed and Lenny. And now Lafe is dead and – and. . .' She broke off, covered her face with her hands.

Pilgrim said nothing, watched her. He was a tough one, a manhunter, could be hard, calculating. Females crying, men begging: he had seen it all before.

Carrie sobbed. From the kitchen came the clatter of crockery. Still covering her face with one hand, Carrie fumbled with the other, got a handkerchief from a small pocket in her shirtwaist. She mopped at her eyes, almost furiously it seemed. But then she looked straight at Pilgrim composing herself, steeling herself. And she talked again.

'Lafe was making a play for me. And I liked him. He was a nice man. A – a strong man. I went out with him a few times. I suppose I told myself there was no harm in it, although I was promised to Ed – everybody said so. But, Joe – but I wasn't sure. . . I hadn't told Ed about my mixed-up feelings, wasn't sure he'd understand. Sometimes I just couldn't make him out. . . .'

'Me neither,' said Pilgrim. And that was the truth. But then he let Carrie go on. She seemed more composed now.

'I have to say that Lafe didn't act right in the saloon. I shouldn't have been there, not even with Ed – I don't really like the place. Maybe the setting gave Lafe the idea that he could act like he did. He didn't seem drunk. But he was bold. He put his arm round my waist.'

Is that all? Pilgrim reflected. And a man had died!

'Ed started yelling at him then. In front of everybody, called him terrible names. Maybe Ed was more suspicious of me and Lafe than I'd thought. Lafe drew his gun, didn't point it right at Ed though, just sort of showed it to him. Then he put it back in its holster and said that if Ed wanted to settle things they could do it outside right then. And he turned and walked towards the batwings.'

Bad, thought Pilgrim, *bad*. In a gunfight Ed

wouldn't have stood a chance against Lafe, who was pretty fast. Pilgrim had seen him in shooting contests, drawing too, and had himself beaten the man, was one of the few who could, maybe. But he had not ever reckoned Ed to be a regular gunny – not like Lafe, although the latter had never actually shot at anybody as far as Pilgrim knew. Ed must have made him pretty damn mad. . . .

Carrie seemed to be getting to the end of her story. Speaking rapidly, then pausing. Then, breathlessly, she went on again. 'Ed drew his knife, said "I'll stop him." I screamed then. "Oh, no," something like that. Ed threw the knife, though. But I think I'd spoiled his aim. He said, "I only wanted to get his arm" . . . .' Her voice faded.

Pilgrim said, 'Then he ran?'

'Yes.'

Arabella must have been half-listening. She came in with the coffee. All three of them were silent then. They sipped the hot brew.

Then Carrie said, 'I must get home. Ma will be wondering what's happened to me.'

'I'll see you through town,' Pilgrim said.

'I'd rather be on my own now, Joe, if you don't mind. I've got the little paint.'

'Yeh, I saw him outside.'

'I'll see you out,' Arabella said.

Carrie lived at the better end of town, before the creek and the willows.

Her father had been killed in a riding accident and Carrie, an only child – a spoiled one, Pilgrim thought – lived with her mother, a seamstress called Ermintrude.

Arabella came back. 'She'll be all right,' she said. 'I think she was telling the truth, Joe. She tried to tell me; but then you turned up.'

'It checks out with what Ed told me,' her husband said. 'But that won't bring Lafe back, will it? Ed seemed to turn into some kind of coward.'

'Well, I suppose you know him better than any of us, honey.'

'Yeh, should do, I guess. But do I know him like I thought I did?'

THREE

The two deputies had not heard anything except the usual town night-noises, fluctuating. A mite louder than usual at times maybe, due probably to things that had happened lately. Bad things. But now nothing seemed menacing. At least, not yet.

Walrus-moustached Pug, the older deputy, was sitting in Pilgrim's chair as he always did when on duty in the marshal's absence. Young Jake had told him to go into his adjacent room and have a lie-down, knowing though that the oldster wouldn't do that.

Jake himself was on a harder chair, a tattered cushion behind his head. The explosion from the rear of the jail threw him out of his seat as if he'd been slammed in the back of the head with a two-by-four. He finished up hands and knees on the floor, moving his spinning head from side to side, slowly, very dazedly, his thick ginger hair flopping over his brow.

He grabbed the edge of the desk to haul himself up slowly. When he could see over the top of the desk, he had a shock. His partner, Pug, was slumped in the armchair with his head back and blood dripping from his chin.

Jake made himself upright, used his hands to help himself around the desk. As he reached Pug, the older man groaned. His thick greying moustache, which he'd grown since he'd quit the prizering and become a lawman, was dappled with blood. His eyes slowly opened, blank at first, then focusing on the white but still handsome face of his partner.

'You all right, son?'

'I think so.' Jake whipped out a bandanna. 'Stay still, *amigo*.' He gently wiped Pug's face, discovering that there was a gash just below the bony cheekbone, the old fighter's weak spot when he was in the ring.

'Somep'n hit me,' Pug said. 'God, will you look at that wall?' He was gazing past Jake then.

The younger man turned his head.

Part of the adobe section between the law-office and jail-cells was leaning, and some of it had crumbled. The wooden door in the centre there, stout though it had been, was now lying flat on the floor. Smoke was still drifting through the shattered gap.

'Gimme that,' Pug said. He took the bloodstained cloth from Jake and holding it to his face, rose to his feet.

Both men negotiated their way around the edge of the desk. Past there they still had to go carefully. Debris littered the floor. The door of Pug's room was wide open, whereas before the explosion it had been closed. But it had not caught the full force of the explosion. The two men didn't pause, but picked their way around the other, stouter, door now lying flat, and through the jagged gap beyond it.

Carrie, on her paint pony, was almost abreast of the law-office when the explosion sounded. Although there was quite a lot of street lighting in this area, the girl saw the red flash above the roof of the jailhouse. Her startled horse reared and the girl was almost thrown from the saddle; but she gripped the reins, regained her equilibrium.

There was nobody near her, though she could see figures moving up ahead on the main street. The explosion had resounded in the town and further into the night.

There was an alley next to the law establishment. From this a horse and rider burst precipitately into view. It was the dead Lafe's brother, Lenny. His face turned towards her then, teeth bared, wild eyes gleaming. And, suddenly, he had a gun in his hand, pointing at the girl.

24

'Ride ahead o' me, Carrie,' he shouted.

Staring blankly, the girl did as she was told.

As she went past Lenny, his horse pawing the ground, the young man fired his gun into the air, setting both his mount and the girl's into a gallop, driving them down the street wildly. Carrie's paint stayed in the lead; folks jumped out of the way, menaced by the flailing hoofs and the gun in the fist of the younker who had a reputation for all kinds of wild behaviour. And there had been that shocking explosion! *What the hell. . . ?*

Pilgrim heard the explosion. Both he and Arabella sprang to their feet. The man told his wife to stay where she was. 'All right,' she said, and he buckled on his gunbelt and left the place.

Outside, he slung the saddle on his horse, urged him fast down the street. The blast had seemed to come from the direction of the jailhouse and, as he approached it, other folk were making for that area, most of them from the other direction, the blustering night-time centre of Willow Flats.

The front of the law-office looked all right. But then, as he dismounted from his horse on the stoop, Pilgrim saw wisps of smoke escaping from under the door. Behind him folks yammered questions. He took no notice of this, unlatched the door, flung it open. Drawing his gun was a reflex action. He didn't know what to expect.

Jake and Pug met him half-way across the office, which was a jumbled mess.

Pug looked as if he had walked into a wall. Jake's eyes didn't look good, but it was he who spoke.

'The back wall's blown in, Joe. Ed's dead. A piece of the bars went right through 'im. Dynamite, we thought.'

'Yeh,' agreed Pug, somewhat blankly.

Pilgrim went past them. He holstered his gun as he picked his way around the fallen communicating door.

He disappeared from the sight of his two deputies. Then he called, 'Give me a hand to get Ed out of here.'

'We should've done that,' muttered Pug, leading the way. The blood was drying on his face, in his whiskers. Jake followed his partner. They knew that Ed Cooley had been an old friend of the marshal's.

Pilgrim shouted, 'One of you go get a blanket.'

Pug turned about. Jake half staggered past him.

As quickly as possible, the deed was done. The remains of Ed Cooley were not good to look on.

A man came through the office door. He had harrowing news. Garbled at first – other folks appearing, yammering – but then frighteningly clear.

It seemed certain that Lenny Trake had caused

the explosion, with dynamite sticks most probably. Then he had kidnapped his late brother's girl, Carrie, and both of them had hit the trail. That seemed about the size of it (would Carrie have gone willingly with Lenny?) and that was the way you had to figure it, seemed like.

Pilgrim barked, 'Get the undertaker to look after Ed. You stay here, Pug, look after that face. You come with me, Jake. I want two more men as well. I want somebody to go see Carrie's ma, pronto – maybe Lenny has dropped her off there after all, was just using her as a shield to get him outa town.'

He hoped that was the truth but, somehow, didn't think it was likely, a feeling he had, not speaking his thoughts aloud.

Folks began to sort themselves out, doing as the marshal said, no argument. The marshal picked two youngish men to go with him and his red-headed deputy, who was more sprightly now that something concrete was being planned. A good young cuss in a pinch, Jake. And the two volunteers, friends of his, were of like stripe.

FOUR

Arabella came riding down the street astride her neat dun mare called Sally. I might've known it, thought Pilgrim. She would have heard those shots: like a pale echo of the explosion, a mite later, as the marshal had been told about it. She would have heard Lenny firing off his gun, driving his horse and the girl's into a wild gallop down main street; Lenny waving his weapon in the air, scaring already mightily alarmed townsfolk.

Pilgrim told his wife things quickly; he couldn't be very reassuring, and had to admit this to himself.

Arabella said, 'I'll have to go and see Carrie's mom. Carrie might be there anyway, Joe.'

'Maybe. Nate is goin' there.' Pilgrim indicated one of the volunteer deputies. 'Come on.' They moved, fast, folks scattering away from them as they went pell-mell down the main street.

28

They paused at a handsome well-lit house. Carrie's ma, Ermintrude, was standing on the porch. Pilgrim wondered whether the woman had seen her daughter and Lenny or whether she had just stepped out to see what all the frightening commotion was about.

She stared at them. Arabella and Nate, a lean young towhead, went up to the elderly lady; and the girl, her dark-gold hair covered by a modish Stetson, approached her closely.

Arabella spoke quickly. The others saw Ermintrude's hand rise to her mouth as she shook her head vigorously from side to side, her eyes wide and wild in the lights.

Young Nate came back down. Arabella waved to her husband, a signal that she was staying with Ermintrude. He nodded briefly and nudged his horse forward, as did the other men.

Pilgrim looked back briefly over his shoulder, not an easy thing to do when at full gallop. He saw the door close behind the two women.

What lay ahead of the posse? A frightened girl alone on the trail? Nothing? Those two had a good start! Would they stay together? Or would something terrible happen? The latter possibility didn't bear thinking about. . . .

What had led things to this pass? Ed Cooley had been a sort of catalyst. And coincidence had paid a big part also.

Joe Pilgrim and Ed Cooley had been boyhood friends back on the Pecos where Joe's parents had run a ranch and Ed's folks a dry-goods store. That was before Joe started a-roving, taking up the profession that had been his father's before he retired from it and took up cattle-raising, the man that most everybody referred to as 'Marshal Joe'.

Young Joe, however, had not toted a law badge as much as his father had. He had been instead a sort of troubleshooter and range detective, always if possible right on the side of the law.

A fast gunhand, a man with a rep. Usually a man like that stopped a bullet sooner or later.

But Joe Pilgrim had met Arabella Teller and her Dad, Pete, and his roaming days had come to an end till friends offered him a badge.

On the other hand, Pilgrim's old schoolmate, Ed Cooley, had come to this territory – Marshal Pilgrim's bailiwick – by other ways and means entirely, and that after Joe had pinned on his silver star.

The undertaker and the doc spotted the fire first. It had been spluttering unnoticed under shattered, fallen timber, and suddenly broke through.

The mutilated body of Ed Cooley was taken away. Pug and a bunch of volunteers took over, Pug with a rather grotesque plaster which the medico had put on the deputy's wounded face. It made the ex-fighter more like the proverbial gargoyle than ever, the sawbones commented.

Doc had a ribald sense of humour. And the undertaker brayed like a donkey at the quip, making his own long and lugubrious face – his professional one – more grotesque than ever.

Willow Flats had a fire-engine and a corps of volunteers, but Pug saw no necessity to send for them: their would-be military procedure was liable to lead to an entanglement of legs, skittering the horses – and by the time they all got to the fire it could have spread.

Chains of buckets were used and what had grown into red and yellow flames became a spluttering section once more, then a smoke that made men cough and, finally, a mucky black turbidity.

The back of the jail would have to be completely rebuilt though, that was for sure. Pug's quarters were in somewhat of a mess. He wished he was with the posse.

Although he couldn't possibly have known this, right now the posse would have welcomed Pug because the ex-fighter had turned out to be a natural tracker. Even better than Pilgrim was, and that was saying something.

Still and all, though, Pug was the marshal's main deputy, his sidekick, having been with that notorious gunfighter longer than young Jake had, or anybody else. So it had been fitting that Pug stay behind ramrodding the town while the marshal and the posse were out on other things, though, in the night now, the trail-seekers weren't doing all that good.

Their quarry, Lenny Trake, was often a drifter in the wild lands, had been accused once of rustling but this hadn't been proved.

He was a wild one, however, and everybody feared for the girl he'd taken away. What would happen to that innocent victim?

A pale sliver of moon gave an eerie light and wisps of cloud scudded across it, creating shifting shadows on the trail which, judging by its condition, wasn't altogether champion even at the best of times.

The lone rider had figured he was going good; but now he wasn't so sure. He had known Willow Flats way back, had had an uncle there, long since dead. That had been a long time ago when he – the rider – had been a wild kid.

He wasn't wild now; he knew better. No, but it would be a hell of a note if he was lost.

He had planned to ride into Willow Flats by night, sort of unobtrusively, to make his meet; but now he wasn't too sure about anything, even meeting anybody surreptitiously, as had been planned.

Ahead of him and sort of over to the right he spotted some small bluffs, black, with fluctuating gleamings – the tricks of the moving clouds and the slice of pale moon.

Although his manoeuvre took him off the vague trail somewhat, he turned his horse's head in the direction of the bluffs. They had come a long way and the beast balked a bit, tiredly.

'Not far now, *amigo*,' said the man and hoped he wasn't talking through his hat.

FIVE

The man and the girl had ridden hard. The man had made the girl go in front of him all the time, reaching out and quirting her horse if she let him lag.

Only when they saw the dark bluffs ahead of them, their image fluctuating in a ghostly manner under the pale moon, did the man move his horse to the side of the other mount, but not too near.

He said, 'Them little hills an' gullies used to be my hideyhole when I was a kid. I guess I found places that nobody else ever did, not even Brother Lafe, though we were together a lot most of the time an' he was the eldest, so sort of the boss. But these were my secret places he didn't know about. Nobody else seemed to come here, except small bunches of Injuns from time to time, an' I kept away from them.'

'Let me go, Lenny,' the girl said. 'Please. This won't do no good.'

The man laughed, not a particularly pleasant sound. 'It might do me some good, sort of. I might let you go when I'm good an' ready. Or I might just leave you here an' you can scream for the posse, lead 'em over here off the trail, while I hit the big yonder. I ain't seen any Injuns in a coon's age but some might wander along. They could have some pretty games with a nice little filly like you.'

'You're crazy,' the girl said, and now she spurred her horse ahead of him.

With a whoop, Lenny went after her. He was all through talking it seemed.

He caught up with her on the edge of the bluff, her horse stumbling on the suddenly rough terrain. He grabbed the reins. She had no quirt like he had, didn't believe in any kind of whip, didn't wear spurs on her boots either. She swung at him with her gloved, balled fist, but he caught it, clutched it tightly.

He almost yanked her out of the saddle. He put his other arm around her, keeping himself in the saddle with the pressure of his knees. He was an accomplished horseman (one of the things he was good at) and his mount was well trained, well treated too – far better than the rider was treating the girl now, his fingers digging into her breast.

She jerked herself violently away from him, and

her startled horse surged forward, his hoofs clattering on loose rocks, small, jagged, round, perilous.

Lenny's horse was then right behind, seemed to be enjoying himself. And his master certainly was, chuckling deep in his throat like an inebriated loon.

They caught up with Carrie's mount, a smaller beast more used to moving sedately in the sunshine than scrabbling over rocks in the mysterious night-times. Suddenly, though, his hooves hit softer ground, a tiny clearing with scrub grass that seemed to shift under the light of the pale moon and its playmates, the scudding clouds.

But Carrie's horse was suddenly alarmed again by the bigger beast, whose rider jerked his reins, forcing the smaller one into a sort of sidelong charge.

The girl was taken by surprise also, thrown sideways. She let go of the reins, her hands flailing. She cried out as she fell. She hit the grass and rolled.

Lenny Trake came down from the saddle. Next moment he was at the girl. 'C'mon, Carrie,' he said. 'You ain't hurt.' Then his voice took on an almost pleading quality. A flow of words. Many of his partners had said he was a sort of gabby cuss.

'Y'know I allus thought you were too good for ol' Lafe. I knew you were sparkin' him on the side. Ed too. I can give you more'n either of them did. But

Lafe didn't have to die an', sooner or later, I'm gonna make sure folks pay for it. An' right now you come first.'

Carrie seemed dazed. But she was coming out of it. She said weakly, 'Let me be, Lenny. Please let me be.'

'Cain't do that, Carrie, you know that. An' c'mon. I ain't got all night. I gotta be on my way.'

His hands were all over her. She thrashed, struggled. But her strength seemed to have become depleted. . . .

The two horses sensed conflict. Separately, they shifted. Their hoofs thudded on the grass, now and then kicking up a small rock. At first neither of them seemed to notice the approach of a third horse, only turning their heads to look when the third rider dismounted as the girl screamed.

The third rider had heard her call out before that. He was a wary man who liked women.

'Let her be,' he said.

His voice was not loud, but it carried in the sudden near-stillness.

Carrie pushed Lenny away from her, and he half rose, his right hand dipping. He was fast. And the girl was near, though not exactly a shield. He could have been hard to hit, foreshortened, bracing himself on one knee, a lesser target, and not too awkward.

His gun, however, was only half out of its holster

when the bullet from the standing man's weapon ploughed into his chest, forcing him backwards to fall in a grotesque, twisted position. The gunshot echoed, died. The horses skittered. The girl scrabbled backwards away from Lenny.

His gun still in his hand, the tall stranger strode forward and got down on one knee in front of Lenny, who was still breathing raggedly, the blood already spreading through his checkered shirt under the flung-back, scuffed leather vest.

Eyes wide under the pale moonlight, Lenny looked up at the man who had brought him down, looked up into the dark, lean, sardonic-eyed face and breathed a name.

'LaVere.'

'Hallo, Lenny,' the stranger said. 'I didn't expect to see you so soon and under such circumstances.'

'We wuz waitin' for you,' Lenny croaked, his voice then fading to a whisper. 'Me an' Lafe. But somep'n went wrong. I . . . I . . . Lafe's dead.'

'Now you're dead, Lenny,' the other man said as the younger man's head fell back and, behind the still bulk, the girl uttered a little cry.

'You're all right now, honey,' the man called LaVere said. 'No more harm will come to you.'

SIX

He had holstered his gun. He had figured which was Lenny's horse – had been – the beast bigger than the girl's paint. He lifted the body and placed it across the saddle. He was effortless, careful. He turned towards Carrie and she said:

'He – he kidnapped me. From Willow Flats.'

She was on her feet, erect, holding herself in, her voice a little shaky.

'You all right?'

'Yes, thank you. He didn't hurt me much. He – he didn't have time.'

'I was kinda making for Willow Flats,' said LaVere.

There was a flavour of the South about his accent. Carrie saw now, his face more definite in the pale moonlight, that he had a slash of black moustache on his upper lip.

He wore a long dust-coat and an ordinary dark-coloured Stetson. But there was something about him that said 'gambler'. He was mighty fast with a gun – she'd seen that. A dangerous man. But she wasn't scared of him as she'd been of Lenny. She almost thought she detected a flavour of Southern old-world courtesy about him.

'Can you ride?' he asked.

'I can.' She demonstrated by climbing into the saddle, her pony docile now.

LaVere mounted, said, 'Lead the way. I'll bring this.' He indicated the horse with the body over the saddle.

They were back on the higgledy-piggledy trail when they saw the small posse and were soon surrounded by its members, delighted to see the girl all in one piece.

She said quickly, 'This gent saved me. He had to shoot Lenny.'

'No chance to do anything else,' her deliverer said. 'He drew on me.'

'That's right,' said Carrie.

Marshal Joe Pilgrim and the newcomer were looking at each other. The latter spoke the marshal's name, all of it, familiarly.

'LaVere,' Pilgrim rejoined. 'Brandon LaVere.'

The rest of the posse stared under the pale moon. They'd probably never heard of a name fancier than that, not in all their born days!

'Let's go,' said Pilgrim, turning his horse about.

Their quest suddenly at an end, they made back for town. Pilgrim led the way. LaVere stayed near the girl just a little way behind, leading the horse with the body.

Carrie pushed her horse forward to Pilgrim's side, and asked him, 'What happened to Ed?'

'He's dead, Carrie. Lenny dynamited the back o' the jail where the cells are, where Ed was. Nothing there now.'

'Lenny didn't tell me.'

'Maybe he wasn't mighty sure his ownself.'

'No-oo.'

'But he pulled it off. He figured he'd avenge his brother I guess. Still, the way the Fates had it, in the end Lenny paid for what he'd done.'

'Mr LaVere saved me.' Carrie threw a grateful glance back at the tall rider bringing up the rear with the third horse and its grim burden. 'You know him, don't you, Joe?'

'Yes. But I didn't expect to see him in these parts. I knew him way back.'

'Lenny knew him. Seemed like he was coming to Willow Flats to meet Ed and Lenny.'

'Do tell.' Pilgrim seemed to be thinking about that. There was silence then except for the slowish thud of hoofs. The few lights of the sleeping town were in sight but there was no need for hurry now.

Carrie's ma, Ermintrude, ran out on her stoop, Pilgrim's Bella right behind her. Things were soon straightened out and the three women went back inside, Bella telling her husband she'd see him later.

The posse began to split up. LaVere asked Pilgrim about a decent place to stay. The marshal told him. They split. There were still wisps of smoke coming from the ruined jail.

The marshal and his deputy, Jake, went in the front and told Pug the good news. 'I'll stay here a while,' the marshal said. 'Bella will find me here when she leaves Carrie an' her ma. You two go get some shut-eye.'

Pug said his jailhouse billet was in a bit of a mess – hell, anybody could see that! – but the way he felt right now he could sleep on a plank.

Jake went back home. In a bit Pilgrim could hear Pug snoring. Bella turned up, said Carrie was going to be all right.

Pilgrim said, 'Let's go home. Nothing to do here. Pug'll wake like a cat if he hears anything.'

'You could've fooled me,' Bella said, glancing at the door sagging off its hinges, from behind which issued sounds as if of a bull buffalo having a hideous nightmare. But she followed Joe out, chuckling when he locked the front door after him: force of habit, he said.

LaVere woke a drowsy old-timer from the depths of his cushioned chair behind the desk in the smallish hotel and said he'd been sent there by the marshal, an old friend of his. 'We brought the missing girl back,' he said and the oldster was delighted, wide-awake then.

'She'll be fine.' The elegant-sounding stranger had a sort of way with him.

'I've got a prime room for you, suh,' said the oldster and, keys in hand, led the way up the stairs.

So far an' so good I guess, LaVere thought, but it was a nuisance the two brothers both getting themselves killed, particularly Ed who'd been the smarter of the two, smooth, cunning. LaVere hadn't yet learned the full story of how Ed got his come-uppance; he was sorry he'd had to kill Lenny. But there hadn't been any other way, the goddam young idiot.

He liked the room the oldster led him to, took the key, locked the door behind him. There was a pitcher of clean water which wasn't too warm. He took a big slug of it, then he undressed and got into the narrow but comfortable bed.

He put his long, specially modified Dragoon Colt under the bed but well within his reach if he leaned over and dropped his hand downwards.

He put his back-up gun, the one he carried in a pouch behind his belt, under his pillow. It was a chunky, short-barrelled – this specially cut – Remington pistol. It didn't have an air-trigger – he didn't aim to blow his ear off, or half his head – but

43

he could be pretty fast with it. He was quick with guns, knives, cards, women. Before going to sleep he thought about the girl called Carrie. . . .

SEVEN

The undertaker, whose name was Killey, had three
bodies in his small ice-house back of his 'establishment' as he always called it. Now, in the morning,
the sun was coming in through a narrow, dusty
window. Killey had talked of blocking this up,
wasn't good for the ice he said, and you got more
heat in these parts than anything else. But a
compassionate man, if with sometimes a ghoulish
sense of humour, he had added that he didn't want
to leave his guests in the pitch blackness but let
them sleep; they wouldn't be there long.

The pitiful remains of Ed Cooley, remnants of a
human body – completely covered; and the corpses
of the Trake brothers, one dead from a deeply
inflicted knife-wound, the other from a bullet.

The inquest, which was but a formality, was
being presided over by Judge Silas Weatherly. He
was a congenial oldster whom everybody called

just 'Judge Silas'. He had moved to Willow Flats after his retirement in order to join his widowed sister who, regretfully, had since passed on herself.

He was now in his eighties but still sharp, an honorary go-between for everything legal, a confidant for all kinds of folks, some of the younger calling him 'Uncle'.

The judge sat in the morning. The three-part funeral was in the afternoon. Everybody was there. And the head lawman, Marshal Pilgrim, was to reflect on that.

Back in the Pecos territory, at school and for a while afterwards, Joe Pilgrim and Ed Cooley had been friends. But then they had both begun fiddle-footing and had lost touch.

During his own travelling and the shenanigans he got himself mixed up in, free-lancing and, occasionally, toting a badge, Pilgrim had heard rumours of Ed Cooley getting mixed up with rough company. Who didn't in those days? Including Pilgrim himself.

Ed didn't seem to have actually turned up on any lawmen's dodgers and, since Pilgrim's appointment as marshal of Willow Flats, nothing had turned up there either – except Ed himself, he having bought a small horse-ranch in the outlying territory and mixed himself financially in a few little businesses in town also.

By this time the two Trake brothers, Lafe and

Lenny, had been in the territory a few months after drifting in as if from no-place.

They had worked as waddies for ranches, including for a while a spell with the holdings of Pete Teller, father of Pilgrim's wife Bella and a good friend to his troubleshooting son-in-law.

Meantime, Ed Cooley had taken up with Bella's old childhood friend, Carrie Dulus who, as she later confessed, couldn't quite make up her mind about him and Lafe Trake, a handsome man with a devil-may-care manner that seemed to impress some of the ladies in town – including fair Carrie herself of course.

Who could have predicted that such trivialities could lead to the violent deaths of three men and a fire that could have engulfed a town had it not been stopped in time?

Many folks must have pondered these questions. And the big funeral was a quiet one.

Miss Carrie Dulus stood arm in arm with her friend, Bella Pilgrim. Carrie's dark head was bent all the time while her golden-haired friend stared ahead with boldness, and occasionally exchanged glances with her husband, who stood a few yards away with his two deputies and the man everybody knew now as Brandon LaVere. A name to remember. And some of them had heard it before.

As folks wended their way back down the slopes of Boot Hill, LaVere was seen to detach himself from the rest and march briskly up the main street, probably to return to his hotel.

As the day got longer there was, of course, the usual after-burial carousing, reaching its climax as the yellow lights blossomed. One by one the law-folks turned up, had a few drinks, didn't meet with any aggravation. But the smooth gambler/gunfighter-type feller who seemed to have become a sort of friend of Pilgrim and Co. was not seen at all that night by any of the drunken revellers, harmless or otherwise.

The two riders skirted the town, couldn't be seen by anybody there, they figured. They went along the side of the creek on the side furthest from the town and where the willows were thick.

They could only see flashes of water from time to time, small patches made to glitter by the sun. The power of the sun was getting less, but there was no breeze.

'Geez-us, how much further?' said one of the men.

'Not far now I reckon,' said his partner. 'I guess I've got my directions right.'

'He ought to've written you a map or somep'n,' the other one grumbled. He was the smaller of the two; and peevish.

The creek curved and the bigger man set his horse at a trot, going straight off, away from the waters and the willows, losing sight of them. The sun was low, waning, darkly red. They saw the buildings ahead of them, etched against the redness. A redness now like dark, dried blood.

They heard the sound of an axe, somebody chopping. But they couldn't see anybody.

The main building was stout, long, one-storeyed, squatting strongly, its rows of windows like staring eyes watching them.

There was a large barn and various outhouses, a corral in which horses grazed, a well with a slung tin bucket, a few chickens picking at stuff in the hard-baked earth of the yard.

The main door, a stout one in the middle of the long house, was a little ajar: they could see the black oblong.

The door was pushed from the other side and a dog's muzzle appeared, then the rest of him. A big mottled brown and grey mongrel with a wolfish look about him and teeth like white knives, bared, a menacing growl issuing deeply from the beast's throat, his eyes red as the sun caught them.

The bigger of the two riders – and he was the biggest by far, a veritable giant – drew his gun with an almost negligent gesture and said, softly; 'Wrap it up, dawg.'

Seeing a fellow being maybe, the beast wagged his tail. The big man got down from the saddle. A face like a bristly gargoyle; eyes in it, though which gleamed with a sort of malicious merriment.

He was known as Big Ade, his first name being Adrian, which his mother chose from a Victorian novel, after she taught herself to read that was.

Anybody who called Ade by his first full moniker was asking for a broken jaw, or worse.

His partner, Jollo, dismounted, short, squat, powerful-looking, face like a discontented box-eyed wild cat. But these two ill-assorted individuals rubbed together fine, though nobody who met them could figure why.

The dog, tail still waving, came forward and Ade bent, patted him. The chopping had ceased. The two visitors looked warily about them. Then a man came round the corner of the house, stripped to the waist, lean but powerful-looking, axe swinging in his hand, saying, 'Hallo, boys.'

'Hallo, chief.'

It was like a chorus.

Brandon LaVere – it was he – grounded his axe and the dog ran to him and jumped up playfully.

'Get inside, Gyppo,' LaVere said, and the hound did as he was told.

As the dog went in, a Mexican woman came out. Plump, comely, plain-faced but with huge, dark eyes, clad in a shirtwaist, faded, flowered, and a long skirt. She had moccasins on her feet and moved well, but came only a little way out of the house and stood eyeing the two visitors shyly, almost fearfully.

'This is Nita, boys,' LaVere said. 'That's what I call her. Short for Juanita. She'll look after us from time to time. She wouldn't show herself until she was sure everything was all right. She'll make coffee while I show you two gents around the place.'

The Mexican girl nodded her head in the direction of each of the visitors and then went back into the house.

LaVere led his visitors round the corner of the house, and big Ade said, 'A nice little spread.'

'A horse ranch,' said LaVere. 'Some prime stock in the corral and some more out on the grass.'

'Prime,' said Ade.

'Prime,' echoed Jollo, far from jolly. Maybe he hated ranches – any kind – and what they might entail.

EIGHT

'Joe Pilgrim,' ejaculated Big Ade, his gruff voice now on a high note. 'Marshal? You didn't figure on that, did you, chief?'

'No, I didn't.'

'Ed Cooley could've told you.'

'Maybe he didn't know that me an' Pilgrim were old acquaintances.'

'He ain't about to tell you anythin' about that now, is he?' said Jollo. 'Unless he crawls outa his grave. Him an' his loco brother.'

'No,' said LaVere. He looked at Ade again, asked, 'The other two boys on their way?'

'Yeh, should be here tomorrow.'

'I don't reckon Pilgrim will know them.'

'Guess not.'

'We can take care of Pilgrim if we have to,' said Jollo.

The Devil's Shake

'Hell, I kinda liked Joe in the old days,' said Ade. 'In the border wars.'

'Yeh, but he ain't no blood-brother of ourn,' retorted Jollo.

LaVere said, 'Joe's gonna do some thinkin' about me, I guess, knowing me like he used to. It's a good job I did a deal with Ed Cooley on this place before he got himself killed. An' over a woman too, so I'm told.'

'Maybe Cooley had Lafe Trake figured wrong on everything an' figured to take his place with you an' this place, him an' his brother.'

'Who knows? Anyway, it's a good job we've got the other two boys a-comin' along.'

'Yeh,' said Big Ade. He laughed gutturally. 'And maybe Joe'll figure you've sort of turned over a new leaf, as the sayin' goes, you runnin' this place an' all now, with me an' Jollo, two old friends o' yourn – Joe knows that. An' the two other boys, like drifters, waddies, joinin' us, muckin' in.'

'Yeh,' said LaVere, flash of white teeth, turning, as if he had sensed that Nita had come out of the back door and was watching them. She disappeared.

'Coffee's ready, boys.' LaVere led the way.

Over his shoulder he said, 'Ed Cooley had other leetle businesses in town an' I'm taking 'em over.'

The two boys got to Willow Flats earlier than they had expected and, in any case, they weren't arranged to meet Big Ade and Jollo till the following day.

They had ridden their horses hard. They were wild boys who liked to ride hard, fast. The one called Remy had in fact done some bronc-busting and, as a change, some pony-racing too. They had known each other since they were tads in short britches. They were wild truants then and they hadn't changed much, just got meaner, and wilder even; gambling, boozing, whoring, stealing, killing; and, as far as they knew, neither of them had a name on a law dodger yet.

They hadn't met Brandon LaVere yet either, were to be introduced to him by Ade and Jollo. They'd heard of LaVere's reputation, of course. It was a formidable one. But it didn't faze them at all, nossir!

Must be somep'n kinda weak about a *hombre* with a fancy name like that'n, Remy's partner, Slick had said. Remy was a mite smarter, didn't say anything. . . .

At first the willows hid the town from their sight with only glimpses here and there of lights as they were jounced in their saddles. Then they reached the gap which was level and hard-packed from the hoofs of countless horses.

They splashed through the narrow, shallow creek and the main street of Willow Flats was right ahead of them.

There was a livery stable on the edge of town; they spotted the swinging lantern right away, the half-open welcoming doors.

Although they didn't know this, the stable was the business and the home of one of the oldest settlers, known to all as Red, though he had lost most of his near-crimson locks long since. He was old but still had a good memory. What he didn't know about Willow Flats wasn't worth knowing, and that wasn't much anyway.

He welcomed the two strangers cheerfully, said he'd see to their horses right good. They asked him a few simple questions and he chortled as he answered, took them outside again and pointed down the street with a gnarled finger, made a few gestures to boot.

The next person who saw Remy and Slick – to talk to this is – was Lody Calliope, the madam of the local bordello. Every town had one, a few offshoots too, and Marshal Joe Pilgrim, hard-bitten realist as he was, accepted the fact, made sure that establishments of this type were well policed. He'd had to admit that Lody kept a tight ship. In fact, he had more trouble with the hole-and-corner dives, and occasional free-for-alls in the main saloon, the Shotgun Place, so dubbed by its owner because in his early days he'd been a shotgun guard on a stagecoach line.

Lody Calliope, who had learned her trade in

New Orleans, supplied her customers with wines which weren't bad; but not whiskey or beer; or tequila, mescal, pulque, or any other outlandish concoction, as she termed these beverages of the border towns.

Remy and Slick never played by any rules except their own, which were enormously flexible. They took the biggest room in the place and had two girls apiece, a sort of 'circus'. And they sent one of the girls, surreptitiously, via the back door, out for booze of their and the girls' choices.

Maybe Lody knew good customers when she saw them; hell, she'd had enough practise. She didn't have her beauty any more but, anyway, she loved money more than anything else, and these two wild boys seemed well britched.

But things got out of hand. . . .

The boys began to chase the girls along the corridors and other customers complained.

Lody intervened and was up-ended, and the boys chased the girls out into the street, the whole bunch as drunk as hoot-owls who'd been at the corn. And this lot had been at whiskey and beer and all of the other stuff that Lody hated so much. To show they weren't particular, the boys had even tried the house wines. Slick, bragging that he'd try anything, had drunk cheap champagne from the shoe of a big blonde called Treasure.

Lody hadn't been paid. All she'd captured was a

splitting headache and a bruised knee. She had two bully-boys but, right now, they weren't any help at all. One was lying in a back room with a broken head after a run-in with the boy called Remy. The other had made himself scarce after Remy's partner, Slick, had threatened to put a bullet in his ass.

Deputy Pug, roused from his cot by the down town noise, buckled on his gunbelt. His two colleagues were off duty.

By the time Pug got on to the street, the boys and girls had disappeared into the Shotgun Place and Lody was sitting on her stoop with her head in her hands. She'd seen some wild ones in her day but those two boys took the biscuit!

There were folks on the street, many of them brought out by the caterwauling, and, full of curiosity, were making their ways to the saloon, as that establishment began to sound like it was about to break at the seams.

Lody, dragging herself out of her despondency, saw that Pug was the only lawman on the street. He was an old friend of hers. Tough though he was, he was certainly no match for the two wild boys, or the girls, who seemed to have gone mad.

Lody rose to her feet and, gathering her voluminous skirts together, ran down the street away from the noise and hastened to find Marshal Pilgrim.

NINE

A neighbour of Pilgrim's, a man with a gammy leg who understandably avoided trouble, had already alerted the marshal, who met Lody just past the jailhouse. They were old friends, as good friends as was possible under the circumstances, treating each other with a sort of grudging respect like jovial sparring partners.

Pilgrim left Lody behind and trotted onwards in his moccasins. He had been planning a quiet night and was now more than a mite disgruntled.

The yelling and caterwauling which came from the interior of the Shotgun Place did nothing to improve his mood.

As he reached the sidewalk adjacent to the batwings a man and two dishevelled girls staggered out in a sort of tangle; the man was Deputy Pug, who squawked, 'Goddam harpies! Go back where you came from!'

He flung the two fillies away from him, one at each side and then, turning, cannoned into Pilgrim.

'Chief!' He only called the marshal by this sobriquet at awkward moments, and this was one of them all right.

Pilgrim turned on the two girls, said, 'Do what the man said.'

One of them with hair that had been treated by something that made her look like a wild canary, dishevelled as she was right then, turned on the younger man and attempted to throw her arms around his neck. Pug grabbed her, feigned a kick at her bustle, and she followed her companion down the street, both of them staggering from side to side as if following a zig zag path that only they could see.

Side by side, the two men shouldered through the batwings.

They walked into a bewildering mêlée.

Behind them somebody shouted, causing them to turn their heads, their hands dropping to their belts. But it was only young Jake, the third lawman who, like his chief, had had his quiet night interrupted by alarm. He burst through the batwings, yelling, 'What in hell's goin' on 'ere?'

A thrown bottle zipped between Pilgrim and Pug and caught Jake on the temple, knocking him backwards through the batwings.

'Go see to him,' Pilgrim ordered, and Pug turned.

The marshal ploughed on, folks giving way to him now. Nobody aimed to argue with Joe while he was in a bad mood and right now he was at full speed and like to bust a gasket.

There were more girls and they seemed to be concentrated higgledy piggledy adjacent to the bar. The proprietor of the saloon, the ex-stagecoach guard called Benny Grabe was in the middle of the mêlée and seemed to be struggling with two young *hombres* whom Pilgrim hadn't seen before.

Benny disappeared and one of the young fellers gave out a shrill war whoop and waved above his head something brown and floppy that looked like a fresh scalp taken by a wild Indian.

It didn't need a genius to divine what this wild article was: it was well known that Benny wore a wig that he'd had made up, not very expertly, by a barber in El Paso.

Benny suddenly rose up from out of the depths, his pink baldness shining under the yellow lights. He grabbed for the wig but the young feller evaded him and tossed the floppy thing to his companion. They were both drunk and having themselves a hell of a time, being shrilly encouraged by the girls who were equally inebriated.

But already townsfolk were moving quickly out of that area, making way for the irate marshal.

Now Pilgrim was wearing his star and that was a bad sign for wrongdoers.

Suddenly that particular area near the bar was occupied only by the boss lawman, the girls, and the two young strangers. And, further back, a passage was opening for Pug, Jake, with a bloodied face, and accompanying them a bristling Lody Calliope.

Then even the girls were jostling each other to give room. And the two boys turned to face the lean man with a star on his breast.

Remy faced him first, his hand near his belt. Then the young man's eyes widened and he suddenly didn't look at all drunk.

'Joe Pilgrim,' he said and he moved both his hands away from his sides, spreading them, the fingers empty, unclasped.

Slick had turned, said, 'Who the hell. . . ?'

'It's Pilgrim,' Remy said.

'What's the matter with you? You gone yaller?' Slick demanded, then added, 'He don't look much to me.'

'Slick,' shouted Remy, warningly. But the other boy was already reaching for his gun, and what had been a rough saloon brawl had suddenly turned into something much worse.

Still and all, though, it was obvious the half-drunk boy didn't stand a chance.

The marshal's draw was a move to marvel at. And his gun was up and over in a glittering arc.

Slick's gun was barely half out of its holster when the steel barrel of Pilgrim's .45 hit him on the side of the head, a beautifully placed blow; and the young man was propelled to the spit-and-sawdust-sprinkled boards.

The Shotgun Place was immeasurably quieter now. Pug and Jake moved forward. The latter's blood, brought forth by a red split on his temple, was drying on his face. Pilgrim turned on him, snapped, 'Get the doc. Get that fixed.'

Jake meekly withdrew. Lody Calliope was shepherding her dishevelled charges away. Pug had taken Remy's gun and a stout knife that the younker had been carrying in the back of his belt.

At instructions from the marshal two barflies picked up the unconscious bulk of Slick. Benny Grabe had gotten his wig back on straight and gone back behind the bar where he found his barman, who had been stunned with the barrel of his own sawn-off shotgun – drawn from under the wooden top, but not swiftly enough – by the truculent Slick.

The cortège moved out, including a crestfallen Remy, and his partner, Slick, still asleep in the arms of two barflies. Pilgrim and Pug brought up the rear, watchful. But folks were now drifting homewards and conversation was almost subdued.

'We ain't got any jailhouse now,' Deputy Pug remarked to his chief. 'Where're we gonna put these two?'

'I'll think o' somep'n.'

The local sawbones came bustling down the street, said, 'I fixed Jake an' sent him home. He'll be all right 'cept for a headache. Let me look at that other young feller.'

TEN

'It's dark as pitch in here,' Slick moaned.

'Easier for your head, bucko,' Remy said.

'It aches like hell.'

'Aw, quit your belly-achin'. That little ol' quack did you proud, white turban an' all. You look like you oughta be runnin' a – what d'yuh call it? – one o' them Eastern cathouses. A harem, that's it!'

'It stinks in here as well,' Slick moaned.

Remy said, 'I heard they had the jailhouse burned down. So they hadda put us someplace, didn't they, in case they want to string us up come mornin'?'

'We didn't kill nobody. Anyway, you should've let me take that Pilgrim feller. I heard o' him. But I didn't think he looked much.'

'So you said. But now you're talkin' like that knock's addled your brains or somep'n. I see'd Pilgrim in action once. I was just a tad but I was on

the run. I'd slugged a fat jasper an' taken his roll. You an' me lost touch for a bit didn't we? This was a little place right on the border, a sort of hideout. Pilgrim caught up with a feller he was after an' braced him. I remember that gunny's moniker — they called him Fast-draw Little Bill on account he wasn't very big. But fast, man. Fast! But not fast enough to match Pilgrim who put a pill plumb in the middle of his forehead. I got outa there. . .'

'I was drunk,' Slick said, painfully.

'Hell, you've got a one-track mind. Can't you get some sleep? I'm goin' to . . . Then as soon as we get a bit o' light I'm gonna find a way outa here.'

'They even took our lucifers. . .'

'Mebbe they thought we'd set the place on fire. . .'

'Hell, what is that smell?'

'Onions. Beets. Molasses. I guess this is a store-house, somep'n like. I'll have a crawl around in a while.'

'Horse-shit!'

'Yeh, could be that,' said Remy humorously.

He was sort of chuckling. But the sound was fading away.

'My head,' Slick moaned softly.

But Remy was already snoring.

Slick must have slept.

When he awoke there was some light in his eyes,

not much, but better than the utter darkness.

He looked towards where Remy had been lying, but Remy wasn't there.

A shadow fell across the pale beam of light, almost blocking it out. Slick looked up into the shadow.

The shadow was Remy and he was up in the roof.

'What yuh doin' up there?' Slick called, the words resounding in his head.

And Remy didn't even reply.

Slick looked about him. A small barn, that was all it was. Unidentifiable rubbish in corners. A straw-strewn floor on which the two boys had been lying. That smell – still not identifiable.

Remy fell in a cloud of dust, lay on his back, swearing. But, when he quit this and looked at Slick, he was grinning. 'Thatched roof up there, mixed with 'dobe like down in Mexico. An old job I guess, and it's wearing away.' He pointed upwards. 'See that hole, bucko? And it's a lot bigger than it was.'

'How'd you get up there?' Slick put his aching cranium back on even keel again.

'The wall. Made of 'dobe and wood and small rocks. A mighty strong job done by somebody way back who knew what he was at. It's worn away now and it's pretty easy to climb.'

Slick gave a harsh laugh and pointed. 'There's a door over there.'

'Don't you think I tried that, idiot? That's fastened tight on the outside. It's been renovated too, I reckon. We'd need a battering ram to get that down – an' where would we be then anyway? No, it'll have to be the wall. It's past dawn, and it'll soon get lighter. C'mon, I'll help you.'

They made it.

The town was quiet.

Remy left his suffering partner behind a rubbish tip which didn't look as if it had been used recently, was rotting and stinking; Slick didn't have the energy left to moan about that.

By devious ways Remy made tracks for the livery stable where Slick and he had left their horses the night before. And luck was with them.

Although Remy wasn't aware of the fact, the old hostler, Red, had been present at the late free-for-all at the Shotgun Place and had been skittled by a carelessly flung item of furniture that he hadn't been able to rightly identify, him being unconscious immediately.

Like so many others, Red had gone to bed with a sore head and didn't wake until his boyish helper turned up in the morning, way past time. And by then Slick had let himself in and commandeered the two horses, though, thoughtfully sardonic young man that he was, he had left some greenbacks on a barrelhead.

And the two partners, the hale and the lame, were on the trail again.

The two deputies, one with a bandaged head and the other with sundry bruises, stood in the remains of the jailhouse and faced their chief, who echoed the words that the bruised deputy, and that was Pug, had just said to him.

'They got out? They've disappeared?'

'Yeh, Joe. They got through a hole in the roof, both of 'em.'

'A hole in the roof,' echoed Pilgrim. 'Both of 'em.'

A smile slowly spread across his worn but handsome face. He whispered the words again. Then he began to chuckle. And this soon grew to a laugh and, finally, he was throwing his head back and, otherwise inarticulate, was literally roaring.

ELEVEN

The two boys had crossed the creek at the usual fording place where the water was very shallow. There had obviously been no need for any sort of a bridge here. Remy was leading the way and he did not go right up the trail but turned left and went along the line of the willows.

Slick followed a little way behind, his bandaged head sunk on his breast, his hat askew.

Remy followed the line of the willows till there were no trees left and the water was obviously deep. But Remy didn't aim to cross again anyway. They couldn't see anything of the town now, and Slick didn't even look, following his partner without any complaint, not even a moaning murmur. And Remy turned away from the creek and hit the longer grass; there was no trail here now, nothing at all. Ahead there were a few clumps of trees and the ground was undulating.

All the time Remy had been setting his mount at a jog, but not going hard enough to leave Slick far behind, maybe pitching out of the saddle if his horse tried to catch up.

They had gone a few miles when Slick seemed to come to his senses. Anyway, he urged his horse forward and caught up with his partner, and spoke.

What he said was, 'I gotta rest, bucko, I really have. I don't think we're being follered, do you? Hell, like we said afore, we didn't kill anybody, did we?'

'No, we didn't, ol' pard. An' I don't think Joe Pilgrim will bother much about us.' Remy pointed ahead. 'We'll try that stand of trees up there.'

They climbed. They hit the trees, wended their horses among them.

Remy had always been a good tracker. He also had eyes like a hovering predator.

He said, 'Don't look like anybody's been through here in a coon's age.' He pointed a finger again. 'What's that?'

It was a sort of hillock covered with moss and trailing branches. Remy got down from his horse. Slick stayed where he was, slumped in the saddle like a blanketed Indian at the end of a long trail.

Remy poked about. Then he said, 'It's an old soddy. Somebody dossed here once upon a time. A damn' hermit maybe.' He disappeared from Slick's view. Then, after a bit, his head poked out like a turtle's. He had his hat in his hand and his black hair was ruffled. 'It ain't too dirty,' he called. 'C'mon in.'

Slick managed to join him, and was soon asleep. At a pump by the stable in Willow Flats, Remy had replenished their canteens. But all they had to eat were some old dry biscuits. Remy got out his makings and rolled himself a quirley. He had lucifers he had stolen from the stables. He lit up, reflecting that he should have robbed a cookhouse or something while he was about his depredations.

Slick began to snore. In the half light he was beginning to look better already.

At the little horse-ranch Brandon LaVere awaited the return of Big Ade and little Jollo after their morning visit to Willow Flats. The dog Gyppo sat at his feet. In the kitchen at the back the Mexican girl, Nita, was clattering about at her chores.

Gyppo rose on his haunches, began to growl. Then he quit this and came up on his four paws, wagging his tail. He wandered to the partly opened door and the man followed him. The two riders could be heard better now; could be seen also. Yapping in a friendly way, the dog ran forward, trotted beside the mounted Big Ade to whom he'd taken quite a shine.

The two men reined in.

'Where're the other two?' LaVere demanded. The

two men dismounted, and told him the tale there and then, taking it in turns.

And the disgruntled LaVere gave them the finality: 'So you don't know where those two are now?'

'No,' said Big Ade.

Jollo said, 'Pilgrim ain't bothered to send a posse out.'

'Why would he?' said LaVere, reflectively. 'But those two boys don't know how to get here, do they?'

'No, we wuz to tell 'em, bring 'em here,' Ade said. 'You figured that was best, didn't you, chief?'

'All right,' snapped the boss-man. He turned. The two men and the dog followed him into the house, Gyppo at Ade's side.

'I've got to go to town anyway,' the chief said. 'We'll have some chow an' then all three of us will go.'

It was some time later. The three of them were in the gambling section of the Shotgun Place. This was around the corner of the long bar. It wasn't a big area like you might find in one of the greater gambling towns of the wild West. But it was adequate for Willow Flats, whose marshal, Pilgrim, though an exceeding tough *hombre*, was no strait-laced judge of all humanity. He didn't even cream anything off the top where nefarious establishments were concerned, as many lawmen did elsewhere.

This saloonkeeper, Benny Grabe, had picked his accoutrements well. A shining roulette wheel, a gaggle of green-baize tables, longer ones for dice and other quick betting ploys (some of them thought up on the spur of the moment) of bewildering variety. Chuck-a-luck, buckin' the tiger, wheeling and dealing and shouting the odds, for instance. Benny would bet on anything. That was his weakness: many said it would be his downfall.

And, right now, Brandon LaVere was here to tell him something like that.

Facing his three visitors over a bare expanse of green baize Benny, head bent, was perusing a paper that LaVere had handed to him. As usual when he was ruffled, the saloon-keeper was scratching his head and his brown wig was askew.

LaVere said, 'It's there in black an' white an' you can't gainsay it.'

Benny wasn't sure what 'gainsay' meant. But it was there in black and white all right and that was a fact: a presage of his doom – or something pretty near to that. He didn't seem to have anything to say. And LaVere went on:

'You lost half of this establishment to the late Ed Cooley on the turn of a card and I'm taking over Cooley's holdings. That was arranged weeks ago when Cooley came to see me up-country. So now I own half of this place and I aim to buy you out.'

'I wasn't aimin' . . .' That was as far as Benny

73

got; LaVere cut in on him.

'I think you will. I think you'll sell to me. What you do afterwards is of no concern to me and my colleagues,' indicating with a gesture Big Ade and Jollo, 'except we won't expect you to cut up rough or work against us underhanded in any way.'

'I wouldn't do that,' said Benny weakly.

He pushed his chair a little way back from the table, his eyes wide. Then he became as if frozen. The double barrel of an ornate-looking little pistol had appeared opposite him. It was held in the fist of LaVere, the gleaming snout resting on the edge of the wood.

'Don't go for that gun,' LaVere snarled.

'I – I wasn't gonna – I swear.' Benny was sweating now, one end of his wig almost covering his left eye. 'I was just sorta givin' myself room. I – I. . . .' His voice faded out.

LaVere lowered the gun beneath the table but didn't pouch it. He turned to Big Ade. 'Go get an unbroken deck o' cards from the bar.'

'Sure, chief.'

The big feller soon lumbered back, tossed the pack on the green table under the yellow lights. LaVere pushed the cards to his other man and said, 'Break 'em.'

Jollo was a squat, powerful man with big hands. But as he did what he'd been told to do, his fingers were as gentle and deft as a girl's.

74

'Shuffle 'em.'

Jollo did this, squared them and, at a gesture from his chief, passed them across the table to Benny.

LaVere said, 'You and I will play a few hands for the finish of this.' He glanced around him searchingly. 'Winner take all. I'll let you deal.'

It was a ploy that was well staged. And now Benny acted like a mechanical man. But gambling was his nature and his passion and he almost seemed to brighten a little as he took up the cards.

Too soon, though, he realized he was facing an expert: cool-handed, cool-eyed, fast as a cougar. And the other two pairs of eyes were watching him all the time with a kind of brooding menace.

He was losing. He licked dry lips. 'I'll sell,' he said. 'I'll sell.'

LaVere showed a flash of white teeth, said, 'You're late making your mind up. Maybe too late.'

Benny didn't want to lose again, the way he'd lost to the late Ed Cooley. After Ed was killed Benny had thought he was sitting pretty. Now he was completely demoralized, his hands shaking, the cards fluttering.

LaVere, with a disdainful gesture, dropped his own cards, scattering them. 'I'm a good-natured cuss really,' he said. 'Ain't I, boys?'

'Sure, chief,' said Big Ade.

'Durn' tootin',' said Jollo.

'I'll give you half of what I figured in the first place. That's fair, isn't it? Better than losing it all, and that's what you're aiming to do I reckon. And you can stay as sort of my major-domo, that's what I'd call you – and you know these folk here better than I do.'

Benny knew he was beaten. This man was a sharper; more skilful than a wise monkey, cunning and completely ruthless. And his boys would do exactly what he told them to do, *anything*, no question.

LaVere took a roll of greenbacks out of a pocket.

'All right,' Benny said.

TWELVE

Slick said he felt a whole lot better as they rode again.

'I figured you'd come out of it,' Remy said. 'Whinin' bastard though you are.'

'That's fightin' talk.'

'Hell, I'm too hungry to fight.'

'All right, I owe you a busted jaw then.' Slick, who, after all, was a tough and exceedingly healthy young character, had thrown his bandage away and laved his wound with cold water, though he hadn't been able to use much of that because their canteens were getting low.

There was a thin gash on his temple covered in dried blood. The breeze cooled it, and the afternoon heat wasn't too bad.

The two of them perked up even more when they spotted the cluster of buildings ahead. But they drew themselves apart and slowed down as they approached the place, warily, like always.

A spiral of smoke came from a chimney, but there was no other sign of life.

The place looked neat. A long main building, one-storeyed. Neat outhouses, also one-storey. A tall barn. A corral with horses, a nice bunch of them.

They took a chance. 'Halloah, the house,' Remy called.

There was no reply. Nothing moved.

The Mexican girl, Nita was in the living-room of the house in the front, when, glancing through the window, she spotted the two riders. She spied on them from behind the curtain. She wondered where Gyppo was – gone a-roaming probably, like he often did, wolf-like.

She moved quickly to the back, out the back door, shutting it behind her so that it wouldn't draw attention.

There were two privies. She went into the older one, which was leaning and battered, not the one she usually visited. It was holed and, through the crevices, she could see the back of the house and also had pretty wide glimpses of the area around and the range behind.

Slick and Remy went through the house, didn't find anybody, and weighed things up. Nobody approached them from anyplace around. Slick went out to his horse and got a gunny sack from the saddle; the two boys filled it with provisions, didn't bother to take anything else of value, except a shotgun that Remy found propped behind a door.

They went out to the horses and led them over to the corral; the curious occupants moved to the fence to meet two strangers of their own kind. Only a few words were exchanged by the two boys.

They opened the corral gate, let the horses out and drove them out back on to the range.

From her hiding place Nita watched them go.

There was nothing she could do but wait.

It was twilight when her boss returned, with him came Big Ade and the dog Gyppo.

Jollo was staying in town to keep an eye on Benny, the erstwhile saloon-keeper who would have to talk turkey to his folk. Jollo would turn up later.

Gyppo had loped along with the two men just the way he used to when his old master, Ed Cooley, went into town. He had kept pace with his giant friend's horse. When they'd got to town he had left the three men in the saloon and gone to visit his old friend, Judge Silas, whose pup he'd been before Ed took him over. All Big Ade had to do was emit a shrill whistle when LaVere and he passed the judge's place going out.

Now Nita told her tale, and Big Ade said, 'That'd

be Remy an' Slick I reckon. Sure as shooting.' He laughed gruffly. 'They found this place after all an' I guess they didn't even know who it belonged to.'

LaVere gave him a sour look. Then the man even laughed, though it wasn't a nice sound.

No, the two horse-thieves had not known to whom the place and the horses belonged, certainly wouldn't have stopped if they had. As far as they were concerned, their planned visiting with Brandon LaVere and his two cohorts was a complete wash-out.

Still, they'd figured they'd got something out of this territory after all.

THIRTEEN

Nate and Beth Cardoza had taken over the managership of the Pilgrim ranch after Joe got under way as marshal of Willow Flats, a job that suited him much better than being a sodbuster, or even a rancher, although his pa, Joe senior, had started his spread on the Pecos after retiring from badge-toting.

But old Joe had been older then than young Joe was now, and it appeared the latter still had some law duties ahead of him, though probably not so much fiddle-footing, with or without a tin star.

Anyway, Joe had a place in town now with his wife Bella, daughter of Pete Teller, the Cardozas' old friend.

The Cardozas had lost their own small spread in a fire very close to the time when young Joe, after marrying Bella, had gotten his spread. The Cardozas, with the help of neighbours, had started rebuilding but, having to replenish perished or runaway stock, had run out of money and, later, Joe Pilgrim's offer had been a godsend.

They found they could run the Pilgrim spread quite well – it wasn't as big as Pete Teller's place for instance – with the help of an elderly Mexican called Romano. He had been a *vaquero* for one of the big *ranchos* over the border before he got a busted leg in a cattle stampede. But, a genial and hardworking character, he suited the Cardozas fine.

Nate had had the croup and, though a mite better, had had a late lie-in with Beth fussing over him. They'd not had any children and, accordingly, were as close as two peas in the same pod. Romano was already out working and, with Nate late up, Beth and he sat opposite each other across the breakfast table. They were talking about the Mexican girl, Nita, who worked at the late Ed Cooley's old horse establishment, soon to be taken over by somebody else, they'd heard.

'She could come an' work for us,' Beth said. 'I could use her, and I think Joe 'ud go for that, don't you, honey?'

'I guess,' said Nate. He wasn't sure whether he wanted another woman about the place, wondered how Romano would feel about that also. But Beth, whom he loved with all his heart, pressed on regardless.

'Lots of folk didn't think Nita should've been there with Ed Cooley.'

'That Injun boy was there,' said Nate. 'Sort of a chaperon. . .'

'He's gone back to his people I heard. . .'

'And Ed had Carrie Dulus. . .'

'Yes, I wonder what Carrie thought. She'd be reminded by some of the biddies back in town. Still,' Beth added, 'I got the impression that Carrie and Ed was sort of coolin' off lately. And look what happened.'

'Yeh, three men dead,' said Nate vehemently. 'Ed, an' the two Trake brothers. Whose fault was that, I ask you?'

'Nobody's I guess,' said Beth with an air of finality.

'All right,' said Nate. 'I'll see what Joe says about having Nita here. I reckon him an' Bella 'ull be visitin' soon, mebbe even today.'

'Seems to me that Joe's got a lot on his plate now.'

'He can handle it.' Nate rose. 'Best go see what Romano's about.'

The elderly Mexican stood with a hoe in his hand. He was turned away from Nate and didn't seem to notice the closing of the door, the other man's slow approach. He was gazing out, and Nate followed the direction of his gaze and saw the bunch of horses moving in the distance, not coming towards the ranch. He knew that Romano had eyes like a hovering winged predator, shading them now with one hand blocking out the slanting sunlight which was getting brighter as the day went on.

The man turned, had obviously been aware of his boss's presence all the time. 'Mebbe a dozen horses,' he said. 'Two riders I guess. Don't look familiar to me. But maybe the horses come from Ed Cooley's old place.'

'I'll get the glasses,' said Nate. He went back into the house and got his binoculars, a new thing, his pride 'n' joy.

He joined Romano. He always had trouble focusing, but he made it, said, 'Two all right. Younkers. One of 'em looks like he had an accident to his jib.'

'Know 'em?'

'No.'

Romano took his turn. He didn't know them either. But they agreed that the horses could have come from the late Cooley's place. Sold through a go-between maybe. 'None of our business,' said Nate. 'An' we've got work to do.'

There were a couple of young strays they had to find. They were in fact going in the direction of the Cooley place when they saw more riders, three of them this time.

Nate Cardoza recognized one of them. 'That's Brandon LaVere,' he said. 'I remember him from years ago. I did hear he was in this territory. I don't know the other two.'

The five people came together, reined in. LaVere's companions were a big man and a small squat one with an unpleasant expression.

Smartypants LaVere greeted Nate by name, and Nate said, 'You've got a good memory.'

'That I have.' But LaVere it seemed had no time now for polite niceties. 'You seen two riders with a bunch of horses?' he asked.

'We have.'

'They stole 'em from my place. Ed Cooley's place which I've taken over, fair an' legitimate.'

Nate turned in the saddle, pointed, 'They went over the rise.'

The three men rode on.

Looking back, Nate and Romano lost sight of them as they galloped into the sun.

'LaVere,' said Romano. 'I heard of him. Never see'd him afore, but I've seen the other two on the border. Big Ade an' his sidekick, called Jollo. Gunslingers.'

'So's LaVere,' said Nate. 'And mighty fast. If those three catch up with the younkers there'll be killings. But there's nothing we can do about that, is there, *amigo*?'

'Nope.' Romano was shading his eyes with his hand. 'Two more riders comin' . . . It's the marshal an' 'is missus.'

There were affable greetings. The two from the

ranch told the lawman what had happened, such as it was. Then Nate said, 'We'll come back to the ranch with you.'

'Then I'll have to ride on,' Marshal Pilgrim said.

'We'll come with you,' Nate said.

'Sure we will,' said Romano.

'Thanks, but it's law business,' said Pilgrim, shortly.

He left Bella with the two men and Beth, who was delighted to see her friend. He rode into the sun.

Part Two

To Take a Town

FOURTEEN

The horses were becoming fractious. They had been let loose from the corral backaways and had gloried in the opportunity to run free. With the guidance of the two cowboys that is: they were kind of used to that. They didn't mind that at all.

But things suddenly seemed to go haywire. They'd been partially corralled again, in a wooded grove where the two men had taken their time. One of the men had slept, hidden, snoring, a noise they'd heard before, hadn't liked much, the still time, the time when they weren't supposed to run.

They weren't wild horses. But there were limits!

Slick's horse threw a shoe. More complications. They all stopped.

Slick was out of the saddle and the horse pawed the ground, wasn't putting his leg straight.

'I'll have to leave him,' the man said. 'Use one o' the others.'

He got his saddle down, and his other stuff. Hasty. Frenetic even. Remy stayed in the saddle, fidgeting impatiently, the uncertain feeling being communicated to his mount.

All the horses became restive. And none of them wanted to be saddled, it seemed.

Slick got really savage, blistered the air with his profanity.

'You ain't havin' any luck lately, are you, pard?' Remy said sardonically. 'Cool down that lip. Sound carries.'

'Go on if you want,' Slick snarled.

'Don't tempt me. Make it quick, though. Maybe somebody's got on our trail by now.'

Slick managed to fix his saddle and other gear on a little dun mare who wasn't as cantankerous as the rest, just frisky; she tried to bite him playfully.

But then they were on their way again.

It was Remy who, looking back, saw the riders in the distance. The sun was going down but visibility was still good. He counted three.

He spurred his horse on, Slick's little mare going neck and neck with him.

But the other horses, though maybe getting into the spirit of things, were then of little help. Too lively now. And at the back Slick's lame horse, not to be driven away, was trying to catch up.

Looking back, Slick realized that the pursuers – and they were certainly that now – were beginning to close the gap. He was even able to recognize them. Two of 'em anyway. He couldn't figure rightly the whyfore and wherefore but decided that the trio had warlike intentions.

Then a rifle spat and, finally, the message was clear, the menace.

They were in a valley now, ahead of them a wooded area. They rode into cover. The horses were blown, less restive. And there was sweet grass here.

'There's on'y three of 'em,' Remy said. 'We've got cover, advantage.'

'What the hell?' said Slick. 'Big Ade. Jollo.'

'And the other one is LaVere,' said Remy.

The trio was made up of campaigners seasoned in this sort of thing. They did not come right on, though at first they pretended to do so. Fast. Remy and Slick, their long guns drawn from saddle scabbards, now tried to draw a bead on one of the other of them. They failed. The three split up suddenly, winged away from each other. Almost as if Ade and Jollo were leaving their leader behind.

But LaVere, though not then going as fast as the other two, was weaving his horse from side to side, a well-trained beast who'd been with his master a long time.

Slick and Remy made their mistakes, took shots, one each at the man in the middle, the leader. And both of the boys missed.

91

And then Ade and Jollo were coming in, were both suddenly nearer than could have seemed possible.

'I'll take Ade,' Slick yelled. Ade was the bigger target, and a mite nearer to the obscenity-shouting Slick who threw two rapid shots, his Winchester kicking like a fractious mule.

Both the boys were on their knees, not as steady as they might have been. Slick missed his target. And Remy didn't hit Jollo either.

And LaVere was working with his handgun, not weaving any more now, sending a blistering hail of lead into the trees.

The boys were outnumbered, if only slightly. But they were also outmanoeuvred and outshot, outclassed enormously by three gunhawks who were far more experienced than they were at this sort of thing. Slugs buzzed round them. Leaves and sharp twigs were propelled in their faces, tore at their clothes. It seemed a miracle that neither of them was yet hit by anything lethal.

Remy, turned, half-crawled, half-scrambled. Slick shouted, 'Where're you goin'?'

'They can have the damn' horses,' Remy yelled back. 'I'm drivin' 'em out. Get outa the way.'

It was Slick's turn to scramble, bullets hissing round his head. Remy was using his rifle again but not pointing it at anything human. He fired it twice into the air; and the horses broke.

They went out of the trees like a tide, and the two boys were grabbing their own mounts.

LaVere, taken completely by surprise, couldn't shoot any more, only just managed to get his own horse out of the way of its stampeding fellows.

Both Big Ade and Jollo quit shooting, thinking maybe that the two horse-thieves were making a desperate ploy, using the stolen beasts as cover. But there was no man clinging to any part of this wildly running horseflesh.

In the mêlée Slick and Remy took two different directions. Maybe Slick, confused after just missing a trampling, actually lost his sense of direction. He burst out of the trees almost in the face of Big Ade, who was taken completely by surprise. His horse reared as if startled by a ghost.

Ade's hand gun shot out of his hand and hit the sod. The big feller almost followed it but managed to stay in the saddle.

His big Colt was on the ground. His rifle was still in its sheath at the side of the saddle. Ade grabbed for his back-up gun, a Smith & Wesson with a cut-down barrel. But this was in a made-up holster in back of his belt and awkward to get at while in the saddle. It was mainly what might be called a saloon sneak-gun and Ade had more than once used it as such.

Slick's mount was going like the wind and its rider was low in the saddle. Then the stampeding horses were getting in the way but slowing down, straggling. Ade saw that LaVere and Jollo had moved closer together and were moving towards the trees, neither of them shooting at anything.

Although, of course, Ade didn't know this, his two partners' quarry had gone right through the trees and out the other side and, as if devils were on his heels, was spurring his horse for the wide blue yonder; no sun now, no stolen horses. Just freedom.

Joe Pilgrim heard the shooting. LaVere and his boys caught up I guess, he thought, urging his horse faster.

The wild horseman came right at him in a red flush that was a sort of reflection of a sun that wasn't there any more.

Pilgrim saw the glint of a gun and he drew his own weapon. The other gun barked and the bullet took Pilgrim's hat off. He aimed, fired, the Colt bucking in his fist. A snap shot, but as accurate as he could make it.

The other man went backwards over his saddle and disappeared from view as the horse came wildly on, passing the lawman and his mount.

Gun in hand, Pilgrim got down from the saddle and walked to the body on the ground. It did not move. Pilgrim recognized the face, which still wore the mark he had given it with the barrel of his gun back in the Shotgun Place in Willow Flats.

But the young face was already being masked by the blood which ran down it from the hole in the middle of the forehead above the staring eyes.

Pilgrim holstered his gun. He bent and closed those eyes.

'Stupid,' he said softly. Then, more vehemently, almost like a curse. '*Stupid!*'

There but for Almighty grace. . . .

Another wild boy who had died so young, so very young. . . .

The horses went past him, more slowly, moving together companionably.

They were followed by the three horsemen.

'Joe.' It was almost a chorus.

'Good shooting, Joe,' one of them added, Pilgrim didn't know which one.

'They're my horses, Joe,' LaVere said. 'I got 'em back.'

'I heard all about it,' Pilgrim said. 'Where's the other boy?'

'He got away,' LaVere said.

FIFTEEN

The body of Slick was put over the saddle of his horse after the beast was cajoled back into the group. The four-man party, with the bunch of horses, started back the way they'd come, LaVere riding beside Pilgrim as if they were old partners, which they'd never been, though they'd never been actual enemies: the fancy gambling man with the quick gun had been too cute for that.

He took the opportunity to tell Pilgrim that he had taken over the late Ed Cooley's holdings in Willow Flats as well as the horse ranch, which the marshal had already known about from Nate Cardoza.

If LaVere was going all legitimate, Pilgrim reflected, what did he still want with his old side-kicks, Big Ade and Jollo? They weren't cowboys, and neither were they horse wranglers. They were gunhands.

Enforcers maybe for the Shotgun Place, though Benny Grabe already had some of those and, according to LaVere, Benny worked for him now.

Benny hadn't had much trouble with the law in the shape of Joe Pilgrim and had kept his cohorts in rein except for minor incidents. Pilgrim had once had to shoot a roisterer's ear off for instance before 'posting' him out of town.

In a few truculent words Jollo passed to the marshal on the trail some more information: the fact that the two horse-thieves, called, it seemed, Remy and Slick (he was the dead one), had also been about to join LaVere but had got sidetracked and stole horses instead, though whether they'd known that those were their prospective boss's horses was a moot point.

LaVere gave Jollo a hard glance which the little cuss pretended not to notice. A nasty little son-bitch, Pilgrim reflected. A killer, and an inveterate troublemaker.

Jollo seemed to be peeved about the fact that the dead Slick's partner, Remy, had gotten away into the wide blue yonder, a fact that didn't seem to be worrying LaVere and Pilgrim at all.

The Pilgrim ranch was reached. Pilgrim left the others and called out Nate, told him what had happened and that he was going to tote a body into town. Romano, called, promised to escort Miz Bella into town later.

All this time the horse that had lost a shoe had tagged along with the bunch. He was left at the Pilgrim place. Romano would fix him up and Big Ade would collect him later.

The bunch went on, Pilgrim bringing up the rear with the horse and the body of its erstwhile rider over the saddle. When they reached the horse ranch LaVere asked the marshal to stop for a cup of coffee but the marshal declined politely. LaVere said he'd see him later in town. What for, Pilgrim wondered?

Reaching Willow Flats in darkness, he took the body to the undertakers' and then went to visit old Judge Silas to tell him what had happened.

Did Joe want any more deputies, the astute oldster wanted to know? If he did he'd get 'em sworn in, Joe promised. He took coffee with his old friend and, when he left the quiet frame-house, ran into Bella and Romano returning.

The small limping Mexican said everything was fine back at the spread. Bella, who hadn't actually spoken to her husband since he'd first left her at the place she called their 'second home' wanted to know anxiously if Joe was 'all right'.

His dark, lean face lit up with one of his rare, flashing smiles and he said he was jim-dandy, which wasn't the exact truth. He couldn't seem to get out of his head the way the boy called Slick had died. So quickly, so damned stupidly! Pilgrim himself, though still feeling young and spry for the most time, had been about Slick's age when he first rode the gun-toting trail. But he had survived – and that seemed such a long time ago.

Now Bella invited Romano to the house for coffee and the old *vaquero* said he'd stay till Joe returned from the jail – such as it was now – to check the breeze with deputies Jake and Pug.

'We'll maybe need some more men,' LaVere said to Big Ade and Jollo. 'But I'll check first of all with Benny to see what he's got.'

'They didn't seem much to me,' growled Jollo. 'Not what I see'd of 'em.'

'Some'll turn. Hell, they like money. Maybe I'll get me a new *segundo*.' LaVere was goading the other two and they knew it, were used to it.

The chief went on: 'I'm going into town now an' I want you two to stay here.'

'I've got to go fetch that hoss,' Ade said.

'Leave that till morning.'

LaVere was soon on his way.

Pale moonlight. Scudding clouds. Yellow light; ghostly. Then deeper darkness.

LaVere was almost at the town when, in the moonlight, somebody took a shot at him. A rifle. The sniper was good but not quite good enough. The slug whipped spitefully past the target's shoulder.

LaVere went low in the saddle, twisted his head. He thought, that small clump o' trees! He drew his handgun, put spurs to his horse, started shooting, leaning low, the muzzle of the pistol near the side of his horse's neck.

There was no retaliatory fire. LaVere thought he heard horse's hoofs but maybe it was only the echoes of his shots. And his horse was getting skittish. . . .

They reached the trees, LaVere knowing that he'd been taking a hell of a chance all along.

There was no sight of anybody. A cloud covered the moon now and LaVere couldn't see anything moving ahead. The marksman – and he hadn't been half bad – had obviously decided he wouldn't take any chances against this quick-shooting fool.

The moon came out again and LaVere looked about him, didn't see anything interesting.

He turned his horse about again and they passed the willows and crossed the shallow creek. The lights of Willow Flats were ahead of them but there was nothing moving yet in the horseman's sight.

Carrie Dulus and her ma, Ermintrude were out on their veranda. They seemed jittery, but then recognized him and Carrie said:

'We thought we heard shots.'

LaVere said, 'Yeh, me too. Didn't see anything, though. Just drunk cowboys shootin' off their guns I guess.'

It was a bit early for cowboys to be drunk. Many of them wouldn't be arriving in town just yet. But the two women seemed to be reassured. And Ermintrude said archly, 'Would you like to come in for coffee, Mr LaVere?'

'I'm sorry, ma'am, I can't do that right now. I have an appointment in town.' That was a half-truth. 'I'll take you up on that later, huh?'

'Surely,' said the buxom woman.

Her daughter said, 'You'd always be welcome.'

I wouldn't mind trying that one, LaVere reflected as he rode on. He knew Carrie looked up to him because he'd saved her from something nasty the other day.

But there'd be plenty of time.

When he got to the stable old Red mentioned shooting. This long-timer had eyes and ears that belied his years. The horseman, dismounting, gave Red the same reply he'd given the two women. Red didn't say whether he accepted that or not.

As he walked down the rutted main street, wobbling somewhat on his high-heeled riding-boots, LaVere suddenly realized what a lucky escape he'd had and how foolhardy he'd been. That wasn't like him at all.

Who would want him dead? Benny Grabe?

He was on his way to Benny right now, anyway.

He went into the Shotgun Place, which wasn't very busy yet. Benny was sitting alone at a table near the end of the bar. He seemed to be playing patience. He didn't seem to notice the visitor, or pretended he didn't. When the visitor halted in front of him he acted surprised.

'Let's go in back,' LaVere said.

'All right.' Benny led the way.

It was quite a spacious and well-appointed room. LaVere looked about him, said sardonically, 'We seem to be doing all right.' Then he asked, 'How long you been sitting out there?'

Benny looked startled. Then he said, 'About an hour I guess.'

'Did you hear any shooting?'

'No. Why?'

LaVere was cagey. 'I heard somebody say there was shooting. Just wild cowboys out-aways, huh?'

'I guess.' Smiling weakly, Benny went behind his desk and sat in his swivel chair.

LaVere let him get away with that, put himself on a chair opposite which wasn't so comfortable. 'How many boys you got working for you?' he asked.

'Huh, half a dozen. An' a few on call.'

'I want to see 'em, one by one. I want to talk to 'em.'

Benny stared at him, then said 'All right.' He rose, went over to the door, opened it, yelled, 'Petey, yuh come here.'

As Benny went back to his desk, a kid with

untidy blond hair came through the door. Benny gave him his instructions and he disappeared again. And, about five minutes later, the first man came in.

SIXTEEN

Big Ade decided he'd go collect the horse from the Pilgrim place where Romano was seeing to it. Jollo said he'd done enough riding for one day, he'd stay put. Ade told him to please himself and went outside and mounted up. The sullen runt got on his nerves sometimes.

Jollo had a bottle. Maybe he'd be in a better mood by the time Ade got back.

The girl Nita was in the warm and spacious kitchen. She spent a lot of time there.

She could hear the horses moving restlessly in the corral. They'd had a taste of freedom; maybe they wanted some more.

She heard other hoofbeats, wondered whether the two men were going out, maybe to meet their boss.

The man called LaVere had treated her pretty well, not like a common servant at all.

Ade was like a big bear and, although Nita figured he could be dangerous, she wasn't scared of him. Her feelings about the little man called Jollo were more mixed. He didn't seem to pay her any attention at all. A strange one, and more dangerous maybe than either Ade or their boss.

She was in a mixed frame of mind, not sure what was going to happen to her. She had grieved for her old boss, Ed Cooley because, in his way (and he'd been a strange two-faced character, she thought) he had been good to her.

She was surprised when Jollo came into the kitchen and she saw that he was drunk.

'You an' me is all alone, honey,' he said, his voice slurred.

She did not back away. She faced him. She asked, 'Where's the big man?'

'He's gone a-riding, honey. He's gone to fetch a horse. He won't be back yet. An' neither will the big chief.'

He seemed to think this was hilarious, began to laugh, swaying from side to side, shaking. 'I forgot me bottle,' he managed to burble, and he turned and staggered back through the communicating door.

Nita breathed an audible sigh of relief. But the relief was short-lived. Jollo came banging back through the door with a bottle in his hand.

He took a swig from it then handed it out to her.

She had to back then. She didn't take the bottle. She got the table between them but he came round it, bottle in one hand, the other, the fingers like talons, reaching for her, clutching. He missed her. But now she had her back against the sink.

'C'mon, honey,' he said. 'Have a big drink. An' then you an' me can have ourselves a time.'

She tried to evade him but he reached for her again and, in doing so, he dropped the bottle and it smashed on the floor, the pungent smell of liquor filling the air, striking it.

'Damn' your hide,' he shouted. 'Now look what you did.' Then with both hands he had her pinned against the cupboard which lay next to the sink.

Her head thrashed from side to side, her thick black hair whipping. The sink was full of crockery. And a fry-pan, a big one, its long handle sticking up.

She grabbed the handle. Jollo had hold of her. The top of her shirtwaist tore. She brought the fry-pan heavily up and over, all the force of her strong right arm behind it.

It struck the side of Jollo's head and he went back against the table and then slumped to the floor. Blood ran from his hairline and down his face. His eyes were closed and he was very still.

Nita didn't know whether she'd killed him or not, but she knew she had to get out of there.

Suddenly he started to make noises, though he

was deathly still. The strange noises, the smell of the booze! Nita became panicky, ran to the back door, flung it open.

There was her own little pony in the lean-to, the saddle hanging, which she took down from the wall. Soon she was in the saddle, on the horse. Yellow light streamed through the kitchen door. There was no sound from in there.

I'll go to Romano, she thought. He was her friend.

She was moving. Then she heard the hoofbeats. Not noise from the corral, no. Two horses coming from the direction of the ranch which was run by Mr and Mrs Cardoza with the help of Romano.

The big man returning with the spare horse! Nita turned her steed about, rode him around the house and on the trail which led to Willow Flats.

LaVere didn't ask any of the *hombres* he interviewed if they knew anything about a bushwhacker who'd been in operation this night.

This wasn't what this meeting was about at all. He'd planned this meeting before the mysterious sniper took a shot at him at the other side of the willowy creek.

He offered some of these *hombres* more money. Some of them – the ones he didn't like, the *outside* men – he didn't offer anything at all. But, as he

met them all one by one, there was no friction. Not
yet anyway.

Not exactly a prime bunch, he thought. Hell, he
could get better.

Benny Grabe didn't say much, didn't have much
of a chance. Afterwards he said 'All right'. He was
using the phrase a lot this night. Did he have something up his sleeve – a hole card, a devil's shake?
Nah! LaVere left the place. As he hit the backward
trail he saw the girl Nita going by on her little pony.
He wondered where she was going. To visit a friend
maybe. He didn't dwell on the question. He didn't
quite know what to do about the girl. . . .

Joe Pilgrim was still in the office when Nita
entered. With the marshal was young deputy Jake.
Old Pug was resting.

The girl said, 'I've got to report something to you,
Mr Pilgrim.'

Her brow clouded. But still very pretty. 'Go
ahead, Nita,' the marshal said gently.

He knew the tenor of things back at his ranch,
the friendship between Nita and Beth, Nate and
Romano. Maybe Nita wanted to talk about that.
But why the worried expression?

'Have you gone loco?' Big Ade demanded.

Jollo shook his head slowly from side to side,
then quit this as it obviously gave him pain. He

was slumped on a kitchen chair. His sparse black hair was matted with blood which was in drying spider trails on his ugly face also.

Ade bent his huge bulk, picked the large fry-pan up from the floor and put it back in the sink.

Jollo was mumbling to himself, something about killing somebody.

'The girl's not here,' Ade said. 'It must've been her pony I heard when I was coming back. She didn't come my way so she must've gone to town. An' you're in trouble. From the chief – an' from the local law I shouldn't wonder. I ought to turn my back on yuh. But you've gotta get out of here. Get on your feet, c'mon!'

But Ade didn't bend to help his partner; and Jollo, gathering his senses together, rose, swaying, went through the communicating door.

'You ought to have that haid fixed,' Ade said but didn't volunteer to do this.

When Jollo came back into the kitchen he had his hat on, and his gun-gear and war-bag. He went through the back door without saying anything to Ade, who stood as if he didn't quite know what to do now.

The man with the Winchester repeating rifle had been watching the place, the back particularly, for that seemed to be where all the activity had been lately. He had got back here quickly from his billet nearer to the town. He had seen the girl leave in a hurry and had moved his position in case anybody was chasing her. This way he'd missed Ade on his return, had only had a fleeting glance at the big man as he went through the back door. Such a big, prime target. He waited. There was a pale moon, not a bad light really.

He squatted in the straggly trees out back of the place. His horse was behind an old mesquite clump, a patient beast, waiting.

There were drawn curtains in the kitchen window but they were thin and the light came through. Jollo, easily recognizable, came out of the back door. The moonlight shone on his face. He looked as if somebody had hit him, and his movements were slow, kind of hoppity. The moonlight shone on the ugly, damaged face as Jollo gingerly lifted his saddle on to his horse's back.

The sniper raised his rifle to his shoulder. He drew a bead. Prime, *Prime*!

He squeezed the trigger.

Jollo's head jerked violently sideways as if it was going to fall off. His body went a split second later, banging into the horse's side so that the beast shied in alarm. And the man's squat body hit the ground and became still.

The sniper half rose but then settled again.

Two birds?

110

But the back door didn't open. Ade was kind of slow sometimes, but he wasn't completely stupid.

The curtain twitched at the kitchen window. The rifleman squeezed the trigger again. Glass smashed and tinkled. There was the flash of moonlight, briefly, on the barrel of a handgun and a bullet whipped through branches a yard or so past the sniper's head. He triggered again. More breaking glass. The curtain twitched but then became still.

SEVENTEEN

'Yeh, I could swear I heard shooting,' said Deputy Jake.

'I think you're right,' said Pilgrim, riding beside him.

They spurred their horses on, and the silhouette of the house came into sight under the moon.

'It came from the back,' Jake yelled.

But Pilgrim was already spurring in front of him, whipping around the corner of the house.

The bushwhacker had heard them coming. He went back to his horse and led him out a little way before mounting up.

The two lawmen, flame spitting at them from the kitchen window, scrambled from their horses, flung themselves down. Jake stifled an involuntary scream as he almost rolled into a body on the ground. The staring dead eyes of the squat hard-case he knew as Jollo gawped at him.

He heard Joe shout; sounded like 'cover me!' Then Joe was hitting the back door in a roll; it gave way, maybe slightly ajar already.

He came into the lamplit kitchen and there was Big Ade turning away from the window, gun lifted. Ade was taken completely by surprise.

'Drop it, Ade,' Pilgrim barked, and the giant dropped his weapon. It hit the crockery and the big fry-pan in the sink with a frightening clatter.

Ade was no big brain, but now he'd recognized his mistake.

'Bushwhacker outside,' he gabbled. 'He got Jollo. I – I thought it was you.'

'C'mon in, Jake,' Pilgrim shouted and, gun in hand, the young deputy came through the door.

'Jollo's daid out there,' he said.

Ade burbled. 'I didn't know who it was – I didn't know. . . .'

'Watch him, Jake,' said Pilgrim. He went outside.

He found the scraggly tree, the untidy clump of cacti. There were subtle signs of a man and a horse having been there. But they were obviously long gone.

Pilgrim returned to the kitchen.

'Did the girl get back to town?' Ade asked.

'She did.'

'I had nothin' to do with what Jollo did. I wasn't here then.'

'We know,' snapped Pilgrim. 'But you sort of blot-

113

ted your copybook anyway, didn't you? You could've killed Jake or me. You're comin' back with us.'

'I – I'm sorry, Joe.'

'I guess you will be.'

On the way back they ran into LaVere on the trail. Talk was brief.

'You can bury the other one,' Pilgrim said curtly. But he added a sardonic 'Watch yourself' as they separated.

LaVere hadn't of course told them that he would have been back a whole lot sooner had he not called in at the Dulus place on the edge of town to share a pot of coffee with flirtatious Carrie and Ermintrude, her equally flirtatious ma.

Although he didn't know it, his pleasant biding in town could have saved him from a rifle-slug in the head from a sniper with a wholesale hate. Even so, the gambling man wasn't nearly so cock-a-hoop now as he'd been earlier that night. He went wary too. And he didn't bury Jollo till the following morning, out near the spot where the bushwhacker had squatted, though the now not so smart man didn't of course know a thing about that.

Since the escape of the two boys, Slick and Remy, from their improvised cell, the marshal had to think of someplace else to put wrongdoers, the actual jail looking to be out of use for a long time yet.

There was a square flat-topped barnlike place not far from the jailhouse where an old fur-trapper used to keep his hides before selling them. He'd gone off on a trip about a year ago and had never come back.

There were still a few hides, scraggy remainders left in the stout adobe-and-wattle building, and they were beginning to smell to high heaven; you could more than just sniff 'em when you went past the place.

Pilgrim had the building emptied and cleaned out, the labouring folk having to wear kerchiefs across their jibs while they did the job. But, after a final swill-down with gallons of well-soaped water, the place was passed as fit for human habitation and was fitted with a bunk below the high window which let in the light, though not too much of that.

The old fur-man had been astute. He'd had a heavy door fitted to his improvised warehouse and bars on the high window, the glass beyond long since broken by stone-throwing tads.

The disgruntled Big Ade was incarcerated in this place until the marshal and old Judge Silas could figure out what to do with him.

The judge eventually decided that as Ade hadn't actually shot anybody and, at the time, had been in fear of losing his own life, he would have a heavy fine slapped on his hide, and more to follow (a spell in the hoosegow if he disturbed the peace) and be under the jurisdiction of his boss, LaVere, who would doubtless come up with the gold.

Brandon LaVere and Big Ade both agreed with the judgement, the latter not having much option. His chief was too busy with his holdings in and around town to worry about law-made trifles. Besides, he needed Ade to do something and, as soon as the giant was free, he would send him a-roaming.

Nita, after staying for a while with Bella Pilgrim, went to the Pilgrim ranch to join Nate and Beth Cardoza and her old friend and countryman, Romano, who welcomed her warmly; she'd be an asset, they said.

Things were mainly back on even keel in Willow Flats, though Benny Grabe, part-owner of the Shotgun Place and little more than a sleeping partner now, wouldn't have agreed with that judgement of things if he were asked. Nobody asked him: seemed like he wasn't important enough now, even for that. And he kept the hate in his heart, and waited for his opportunities, *looked* for them, and forced himself to bide his time.

There was an atmosphere of pace in the town which, folks thought, was sorely needed after the things that had happened in recent time, so much at once, far more in fact than had happened since Joe Pilgrim had been marshal. There had been wild doings for a time in the earlier days when Joe first took over. But he'd handled everything that came his way with a cool expertise, mixed every now and then with a calculated savagery. Nobody mixed with Joe.

He had handled the recent things also. Things were still happening, interesting things; nobody but the protagonists knew where those things might lead.

It was revealed, piece by piece, that the late Ed Cooley had had his fingers in more pies in town than anybody had expected, except his friend, one Lawyer Blaggs – that was what everybody called him – who, anyway, was as close-mouthed as an old mule with a broken jaw.

The new man with the fancy name had taken over all Ed's holdings, including the horse ranch outside of town. The ranch had never had a name, still didn't have. But establishments in town had signs erected above to the likes of 'Brandon LaVere, proprietor'. A general stores, a gunsmiths, a shop that sold ladies doodas, a small hotel, the stables. . . .

Old Red, the hostler, was heard to say he didn't care who owned the place, Cooley or LaVere, as long as they didn't give him any grief to make his once flaming thatch any thinner and greyer than it already was. He even referred to LaVere as a Southern 'genulman', though other folks might be in two minds about that, particularly those who knew his rep as a gambling- and gun-artiste.

There was a rumour that LaVere had wanted to take over Madam Lody Calliope's establishment but that she'd put a flea in his ear. That was something that Ed Cooley hadn't had a hand in. It had been Lody's place ever since she moved down from New Orleans where she'd been 'a top girl', and, using her poke well in more ways than a few, had taken over a disused two-storey clapboard building on the edge of town, not on the creek side, and discreetly placed, and had it renovated.

Few folks remembered what the place had been in the past, but it certainly made a fine cathouse.

LaVere was seeing a lot of Carrie Dulus, who was a popular girl. Folks who couldn't see much further than the front of their face looked benignly on the affair. LaVere had charm: there was no gainsaying that. He was becoming part of the town. Even folks who had had misgivings about him were beginning to look at him in a new light: maybe he was forsaking his old ways and becoming eminently 'respectable'.

Things were going Brandon's way all right. With a few rough bits here and there things were going just the way he wanted them.

The boys, shepherded by Big Ade, were coming

in from all over, singly or in pairs, never more than two at a time because that was the way their scheming boss wanted it – and most of them knew him of old, knew him as ruthless but reliable.

They were steered to the horse ranch. LaVere didn't want another series of incidents like those that had happened with Slick and Remy, who had tried to 'hurraw' the town.

A few boys filtered into town, later, one by one, at his behest. But he already had boys in town anyway. At the Shotgun Place. He paid them better than Ed Cooley and Benny Grabe had ever done; and, besides, Benny spent most of his time now at the gambling tables with a tot of rotgut at his elbow. Though he never actually seemed to get completely pie-eyed.

LaVere was a mite mixed up about Benny, though he wouldn't have admitted the fact to anybody but himself. He (Brandon) hadn't been shot at again by any would-be bushwhacker. He'd wondered, of course, whether Benny had been behind the first time – and the killing of Jollo. If so, however, he couldn't see Benny doing the job himself. Benny was a schemer not a doer and, by accounts, wasn't a 'shooting' man at all but somebody who hired other folk to do things like that for him. One of his boys? LaVere had one in particular in mind.

This was a feller called Pecos Dave who had been

what you might call Benny's right-hand man till LaVere happened along.

He was youngish and saturnine and tall and lean, had had a hot rep back in the Pecos before he'd run out from there, some folks said.

He sported twin guns, slung low on his lean frame. He had a sardonic go-to-hell manner and always called LaVere 'boss,' with a little smile.

There was no doubt that he was good with weapons. The twin pistols, the Bowie he kept in the back of his belt. And, most of all, the shining new Winchester repeating rifle ensconced in its fine hide scabbard at the side of his saddle when he went out a-riding.

So there was Pecos Dave. And there was Marshal Joe Pilgrim.

But Joe could never be a bushwhacker, LaVere was plumb sure of that. He knew Joe well enough, the man and his strange, straight-ace codes. He (Brandon) could get Joe fixed. Joe was in the way, could put more than a crimp in Brandon's deep-laid plans. To take over a town and make it dance on its hind legs to *his* tune.

Joe Pilgrim didn't dance to any tune but his own. Brandon had to stop him. It was something that, ultimately, he would have to do himself. There were other ways. But now he balked. . . .

Himself and Joe, just two of 'em, that was the way it would have to be. Maybe things had at last come full circle: maybe that was the way it had always had to be. A pistolero's end for one of them before watchers in a dusty street.

EIGHTEEN

Judge Silas Weatherly was in his kitchen mixing himself a hot grog when he heard the scraping at the door, and the whining. He opened the back door. The dog was right outside, one of his front paws held up, as if greeting his old friend and at the same time showing him things weren't quite as they should be.

'Gyppo,' Judge Silas exclaimed. 'What happened to you? Come in, ol' boy.'

He backed. The dog followed him into the comfortable brightly lit kitchen. He limped, and Silas saw that there was blood above the injured leg, the stuff mingled with mud and fragments of brush and dried grass.

The injured beast made unerringly towards a spot in the corner where there was a cupboard, its door slightly ajar. It was quite a time since that door had closed properly.

Before Silas could reach out to help, Gyppo opened the door wider with his nose.

There was a thick cardboard box in there with a folded blanket in its bottom.

The box crumpled at the sides as the dog lay down, not in it but on top of it. But the thickness of the cloth beneath cushioned him and even the cardboard seemed to fit around him.

This was Gyppo's billet when he visited his old master, his old friend, particularly when he decided to stay overnight instead of returning to the horse ranch.

It had been his bed when he was a pup, after Judge Silas had found him starving out on the prairie, lying at the side of his dead mother who, half wild, had picked up some pestilence that saw the end of her. But the middle-aged childless widower had taken the thin, furry waif home and nursed him and fed him and made him well.

After that the pup, called Gyppo, had grown quickly, powerfully, and Silas had realized this wasn't a town dog, this was an outdoor beast who should be in the open a lot and free to roam.

Ed Cooley had wanted a watch-dog for his horse ranch and had been glad to take the beast over.

The judge had kept the blanketed box in the cupboard, maybe only for sentimental reasons in his old age, as he'd chided himself. But, without an invite, Gyppo started a-visiting; his old billet still remained and was being used from time to time.

'You stay there a mite, ol' boy,' Silas told him. 'I'll go fetch Randy.'

Randy Collen, the local vet, was about the same age as the judge and lived only a few doors away. He soon came back with his old friend.

Gyppo knew Randy too and limped out of the cupboard to greet him.

'Who would do that to you, boy?' Randy said, getting down on one knee before the injured animal who licked his face. 'Who would do that?' The elderly vet's love for animals of all kinds was a palpable and heart-warming thing.

He delved into the large satchel that he'd brought with him. 'Hot water,' he said.

'Won't take a minute,' said Silas.

Gyppo was with two old friends, no problem.

'He's been shot,' said Randy eventually. 'Look! The bullet went right through.'

'Who would. . . ?' Silas left the sentence unfinished.

'I'll fix him now. Look. Then I'll take him back to my place.'

'All right.'

And they were soon gone, Randy and his charge, as docile as an infant.

Who? thought Silas again. Maybe he could find out. He tidied himself up. He went down the street to the Shotgun Place.

He found what he was looking for. Two folk in fact. Brandon LaVere and his chunky side-kick, Jollo. There was no sign of Big Ade.

The two men were sitting with Benny Grabe and one of his cohorts, the tall, lean one called Pecos Dave. They had cards on the green baize before them but didn't seem to be actually playing. In fact, they seemed to be having an argument.

Silas heard LaVere say, 'I've got to find out.' But then the judge was upon them, looking up at him, surprised to see him as he didn't come into this place very often.

'Want to take a hand, Judge?' said Benny, shifty-eyed, licking dry lips, trying to be funny and not making it.

'I want to talk to Brandon,' the judge said. 'The dog Gyppo came to me. Somebody shot him.'

'How. . . ?' LaVere seemed at a loss for words, unusual for him. But Silas waited a moment, and the younger man went on. 'I thought Gyppo was back at the place with Ade. That hound's taken quite a shine to the big feller.'

'The dog's with the vet,' Silas said. 'Randy says he thinks he's going to be all right. You'll have to go see.'

'I will. Thank you for telling me.'

'That's all right.' Silas turned away, began to wend his way through the growing crowd towards the batwings. He heard LaVere's voice raised behind him.

'I haven't finished with you yet.'

He turned. But the fancy man wasn't addressing him. His eyes were on Pecos Dave, who seemed to be moving away from the table, making for a nearby side-door. The lean man stopped, turned, a sneering smile on his face. But then he said 'All right' and turned back.

The judge noticed two young hard-looking youngsters he didn't think he'd seen before turn away from the bar as if to move towards the table. He thought he saw LaVere give them a signal, a sort of quick, small wave of the hand. They turned away again.

Pecos Dave had reseated himself. Judge Silas went on, folks exchanging greetings or 'goodnights' with him, as they had when he came in. He went back through the swinging doors. He wasn't happy. Things are brewing, he thought. . . .

Pilgrim and Pug sat in the law office. Behind them was the sound of hammering. The builders were working late, using what light filtered through from the front, so great were the gaps, and tar-daubed flaming torches gave a fluctuating macabre touch to the scene. After school-time they'd been plagued by kids, but these were all in bed now. There were interested townies though, giving a hand from time to time.

Pilgrim had been using Pug as a kind of sounding-board, as he sometimes did. And the walrus-moustached old-timer said now, 'Red would do it, I reckon.'

Pilgrim said, 'The only Red I know in town is the old-timer at the stables.'

'That's the one. He's an old Injun fighter. And the best tracker I've ever known. Better than you even, bucko.'

Pilgrim said, 'I know plenty folk better'n me at that – an' that's a fact.'

Pug said, 'When I quit the fight game and first came to this territory I worked for a time with your father-in-law, Pete Teller, at his spread. . .'

'Yeh, you told me.'

'Red was there then,' Pug went on. 'Waddyin' at a drive like I was, though neither of us had done any cowpunchin' before. So we sorta gravitated together, y'see. We had trouble from a pack o' wolves led by the biggest critter of that kind I've ever seen. Me an' Red went after the brute. Red tracked 'im. Crawlin' on our bellies most of the time. We got 'im! Put some shot among the others as well. We got rid of 'em.'

Pilgrim said, 'That was years ago.'

'Not so long, really. And Red's still a fit man. Does a lotta roaming, leaving that kid to look after the place for him. His nephew, I think. A good kid . . . . I think Red would do it, Joe.'

'All right. Broach him then. And, if he's interested, bring him down here.'

'Shall I go now?'

'Sure, why not?'

As Pug went out, his young partner, Jake, came in. They sparred playfully. The door closed. Jake took the chair that Pug had vacated and said, 'More new faces in town.'

'Yeh, I've seen a few.'

'Where's Pug goin' in such an all-fired hurry?'

Pilgrim grinned. 'When he gets back all will be told.'

NINETEEN

Pecos Dave took the usual trail out of town, across the creek and past the willows, which most people took coming or going, unless they were on the other side of town. Men, for instance, who didn't want folks to know that they used the cathouse or some other place, hole and corner. That was what some folk called the 'shady' end of town, and there wasn't much past there except scrub, sand, rocks, and prickly plants for some miles with only a few smallholdings, which for the most part weren't well run and could be cover for nefarious doings.

But Pecos Dave knew the main trail well. Hadn't Ed Cooley been one of his bosses before Ed got himself killed? Dave had visited Ed many a time at the horse ranch, had liked Ed far more than he'd ever liked the other 'boss', the bewigged Benny Grabe.

So Dave, a shooter, had kept his nose clean. Oh,

129

he could use his gear all right, had killed with it. But he didn't have his moniker on any law dodgers and, all in all, had been sitting kinda pretty.

Two guns or not – and the very sight of 'em scared some folk – Dave knew his limitations. He knew he would not stand much of a chance in a stand-up shoot-out with Marshal Pilgrim. Same went for LaVere, another man with a formidable rep.

There were other ways, of course.

Still an' all. . . .

He knew LaVere was full of suspicions. He knew LaVere was testing him now. He had to go to the horse ranch and join with Big Ade, to help that ape look after 'certain new arrivals', that was what LaVere had called them.

Was Pecos Dave to be a replacement for Ade's dead partner, Jollo?

He didn't know whether that would sit well with him or not. But, for the time being, he got a sort of malicious satisfaction out of following orders.

A thick-haired, pale-eyed young feller he had never seen before stopped him at the ranch with a shotgun, but backed off when Dave told him that he'd had orders from LaVere to come see Big Ade. Then Ade was at the door beckoning him in. And the younger feller, though easing away, was still looking at the new arrival with a leer on his face now, which Dave didn't like the look of at all.

*

Hostler Red wasn't far behind Pecos Dave, though not seen by him. When Red didn't want to be seen he was plumb invisible.

He saw Dave enter the house at the horse ranch with Big Ade and another feller, younger. Red didn't think he'd seen this young feller. Fixed as he was, the stable being right on the edge of town off the main trail, he saw most everybody come in, and some of them left their cayuses with him.

There'd been more than a few new arrivals lately.

He had fallen in easily with Marshal Joe's plan: to keep an eye on the horse ranch, on LaVere and his folk. Red didn't like that fancy bastard much, didn't trust him.

Anyway, this was like old times, reminding him of the time Pug and he went wolf-hunting, something that his old friend, now a smart ass law deputy, had reminded him of. They'd joshed each other like always and Red had acted reluctant. But he'd agreed eventually as, of course, he'd decided to do all along. Joe Pilgrim would pay him well for his time, and Red's kid would look after the stable, had had to do that quite a lot at night when Red was in the Shotgun Place.

Now the hostler made a wide detour of the house and came in at the back, keeping his eyes peeled all the time in the pale moonlight.

He didn't see anybody else. There were lights glimmering inside the house.

LaVere was late leaving the Shotgun Place. He could have stayed there. Benny had fixed a fine room for him, though LaVere thought that that cuss had other things on his mind also. Besides, LaVere had other plans back there at the home place.

He took a roundabout way, though, crossing the shallow stream higher up than usual, out of sight of the few lights that were still on in the town, and having to guide his horse through the willows. Then he'd turned left as always. But he'd still continued to detour. He came at the house from the back.

He did not know he was being watched.

He did not know that, after he'd entered the house, the kitchen door closing behind him, two people were watching, neither of whom saw the other.

A bit earlier one of them out there had seen something that he hadn't expected to see. But, after that, seeing LaVere turn up was no surprise at all.

The kitchen lamp blossomed, making LaVere blink, his hand going down instinctively to his gunbutt, easing, though. Big Ade stood there, blinking owlishly, alone, saying, 'Hallo, chief.'

LaVere didn't return the greeting, asked, 'Pecos Dave here?'

'He is. Been here some time.'

'Where is he?'

'In the lean-to.' Ade pointed a stubby finger past his boss, raised that hand and scratched his head, then said:

'I don't reckon he was the one.'

'Yeh, I was beginning to have doubts myself,' LaVere said. 'He's a show-off, flashy twin guns an' all that. Fancy rifle, which I'm told he can use pretty good. He'll bluster, and that scares some folks. But he'll back down eventually if you push him.'

Ade cackled, 'We pushed him, me an' Loopy.'

Ade jerked a thumb. 'In the other room. I told him to stay there. He liked it. He wanted to join in. He used some tricks on Dave that I couldn't have thought up.'

'One-track mind an' one-track fists,' LaVere snorted. 'Damn it, Ade, I told you to handle it yourself.'

'Well, Loopy wanted. . .'

'Call him in here. Go on!'

'All right, chief.' Ade went back through the communicating door, soon returned with the blond haired kid with pale eyes, who said, 'Hallo, Mr LaVere.'

The rancher didn't reply, strode forward. But

133

Loopy, who obviously wasn't too bright, misinterpreted the move and held out his hand for a shake. LaVere's hand came up but it was swift, balled into a fist. And the knuckles drove into Loopy's loose mouth with savage force. The younker was driven back hard into the door which was partly open behind him, forcing it wide open. He went through it, his legs kicking up.

He sprawled there under the light, his strange eyes now glazed, his face sort of lop-sided, blood running down his chin and spattering his shirt-front. He wasn't completely unconscious, however, and his burst lips moved, tried to find words.

LaVere bent over him, said softly, 'I was gonna hire you. Now I'm not. You don't horn in on my business. I want you to get your gear together and get out of here. If I see you around these parts again I'll have you shot.' He turned to the big fellow who stood stupidly at the communicating door, his bulk half in half out of the kitchen. 'See to it, Ade. Then I want Pecos Dave brought in.'

'All right, chief. I'm sorry. . .'

'Do it!'

The jailhouse, what there was left of it, didn't need watching any more. Anyway, the builders were still working by torchlight in the back. The marshal and his two deputies left them to it and went for a *pasear* downtown. Things were closing down.

Lights were going off. But this was often when the bad times started. And there might be wild strangers around again.

There were still lights on in the Shotgun Place.

The three of them went through the batwings, Pilgrim in the middle.

There weren't many folks in there and some were on their way out, jostling the three lawmen, exchanging sleepy or jovial 'goodnights'.

There were a few customers at the bar and some others in relaxed attitudes in the gaming area.

The visitors didn't spot Benny Grabe right off. But then there was some noise from down in the gaming section and the attention of the three men was driven to there. And there was Benny at a table, his head right on it, in fact. And there were two fellows, strangers, poking at him, mocking him.

'What's the trouble, boys?' the marshal said. The two youngish, hard-looking characters turned their heads, and one of them said:

'We wuz tryin' to wake this ol' goat up. He owes us money.'

'Stand away,' said Pilgrim, and they did what they were told.

Pilgrim gripped Benny's shoulder and tried to lift him. Benny's wig fell off into a pool of liquor on the table-top.

'You boys workin' around here?' Pilgrim asked, ignoring the sniggers.

135

'We're gonna work for Mr LaVere,' one of them said.

'Do you know where the law-office is?' Pilgrim asked.

'We thought it was burned.' More sniggers. But the tall gent they knew as the marshal, though right now he wore no star, didn't seem amused. Joe Pilgrim. They'd been told about him.

'Yeh,' one of them said.

And the marshal said, 'Be at the law-office tomorrow and if there's any money comin' to you, you'll get it. I'll check with Benny. Now goodnight.'

One said 'goodnight'. The other just scowled. They left.

Pilgrim said, 'Get 'im to bed.'

Pug said, 'He sort of had the stuffin' knocked outa him, I reckon.' Jake and he wrestled with Benny who was starting to mutter to himself.

'He's no match for LaVere at that,' Pilgrim said. 'An' I think LaVere thinks he might be takin' a town. And some places outside of it too, I shouldn't wonder.'

He watched his two deputies as they managed to lug the now owlishly protesting Benny to his feet.

And the marshal added, as if apropos of nothing, 'It's been tried before.'

He put Benny's wig back on the bald, nodding head. The sodden top-piece stank of stale whiskey.

Benny, walking cross-legged now, began to lick his lips, and drool ran down his chin.

Pecos Dave was sitting against the wall in the corner of the lean-to when Ade opened the door. Ade took his big knife from the back of his belt, and Dave said:

'Whyn't you just shoot me?'

Ade guffawed. 'It'd make too much noise.'

He reached the other man. Dave flinched as the huge bulk bent over him. As his hands and legs were bound, Dave couldn't do much more than cringe.

Ade cut the bonds and said, 'The chief wants to see you. An' don't worry about Loopy, he's gone. An' he won't come back.'

Hostler Red saw Ade shepherd Pecos Dave across the sod. Dave was mighty unsteady on his feet and, under the pale moon, his face looked as if it had been trampled on by playful buffaloes. All told, he was pretty raggedy-looking.

The kitchen door closed behind the two men.

Red heard the hoofbeats on the other side of the house, coming fast, and he went round the side, keeping close to the wall.

He saw the two new men dismount from their steeds and go through the front door. Red stayed where he was, silent as a cat waiting to pounce.

TWENTY

The young sadist called Loopy had heard the two riders coming and had pulled aside, stayed doggo till they'd gone by. Then he moved on to the trail again. The trail to Willow Flats.

Fancypants LaVere had told him, on pain of death, to take his ass right outa this territory. But Loopy didn't aim to do that. Not yet anyway.

His jaw ached like hell but he didn't think it was broken. Every time his horse hit a bump of ground, though, the pain shot up into the top of Loopy's head like a shooting, searing flame. Maybe I ought to see the doc, he thought.

But, sure as hell, that wasn't the real reason he was going to town.

He had a partner; Loopy hoped he still was, anyway: he hadn't been one of the riders who'd just passed, had promised to wait in fact. An old partner; and Loopy aimed to tell him that neither of 'em needed LaVere; they would be all right on their own, as they'd been before. LaVere was a snake: they couldn't trust him.

His partner, name of Daggert, was sitting on a bench on the stoop outside the Shotgun Place, which looked quiet.

'What happened to you?' Daggert wanted to know. Loopy told him. Daggert said Loopy oughta go see the doc.

The doc wasn't pleased about being wakened in the middle of the night by two hard-looking young men he didn't think he knew, one half-drunk, the other looking as if he'd been kicked by a horse. He was a compassionate and conscientious old body, though, was the doc, and he fitted Loopy up to look like an old man with the toothache.

'We'll leave in the mornin',' Loopy said to Daggert, and Daggert agreed. Loopy had always been the forceful one of the pair. They found an empty lean-to at the side of a general store and they dossed down there.

Big Ade had fixed Pecos Dave up pretty good under the yellow light. Dave sort of went to sleep as the job was almost finished and the others left him in the battered armchair and found themselves little billets in the room. None of them wanted to go to bed, it seemed: Ade, LaVere, and the two new arrivals, both of them of about the same age as the damaged, though now more presentable Pecos Dave. Only thing was he snored like a buzz-saw and one of the boys put a cushion against his face till he shut up.

'Don't stifle 'im after all the trouble I took,' Big Ade said.

But after that Dave slept like a babe, and when he woke up LaVere was bending over him.

'You're my man now, huh, bucko, we agreed on that,' he said. 'You're not Benny's. Benny's gonna be gone.'

'Benny's gonna be gone,' Dave echoed drowsily.

'Get up then. I want you gone. Ade's got your guns, your gear. He'll come along with you.'

'Breakfast. . . ?'

'Now don't be goddam cheeky.'

It was still not quite light.

Like a silently lurking cougar, hostler Red watched the two men go.

I ought to be going again myself soon, Red reflected – or I might even get spotted. Besides, he'd have to tell Joe Pilgrim what was going on, mysterious though it all seemed to be so far but, then again, too many folk were toing and froing, not a good sign, not a good sign at all. LaVere was a fox who was gathering in most of the dangerous cubs together, and that couldn't be good news for Willow Flats, the way Red saw it.

Willow Flats had been his bailiwick for a long, long time, had seen a few bad times before Marshal

Pilgrim appeared, Red's friend and sometimes his mentor. . . .

Red had a feeling of urgency. There was something else too, something that had been coming on in the latter part of the night. But nothing firm; so that he put the feeling down as something of imagination, though he'd never thought of himself as a man with any imagination at all, had thought of himself as a practical man who went about his business quietly, without drama or jabber or showing off. He was good at what he did. With horses, sometimes with men, and with the trails. As solemn as a trailing Injun!

But the feeling was a feeling of being *watched*; and it was getting stronger.

He went back to get his horse. The beast was a fair distance from the back of the house and well hidden, a patient cayuse who was used to waiting. But now Red heard him moving restlessly before he reached him. And Red dropped his hand to the butt of his gun in the old low-slung holster.

The man was going back through the trees. And Red said 'Hold it.'

The man turned. He had a rifle in his hand. He lifted it.

Red drew his gun. He was no artiste, but he was pretty fast. But the other man fired first and Red saw his startled eyes: he'd been quick. Too quick! The slug took Red's hat off.

Red fired back. He hit! The man staggered, dropping his rifle. The eyes became wild as if in protest. The man was falling, helplessly. Red knew he didn't have to fire again.

He had seen men die violently before. It sent a pain to his heart.

He was still standing when the men came out of the house towards him. He was almost trancelike, holstering his gun as he turned.

Three men. In the lead was LaVere, a gun in his hand. The two men behind him were younger. They both had guns out but, with a half turn of his head, their leader barked, 'Put 'em away,' and they did so.

Red's head was straight again. He even bent and picked up his hat. He said, 'I was out early riding like I do sometimes when I can't sleep. I'm no late sleeper.' He pointed. 'He came out at me, took a shot at me.' He poked a finger through the hole in the crown of his Stetson.

All they could see were the boots of the man lying in the tangled scrub which might have been his hiding place.

Or one of his hiding places.

LaVere had nonchalantly holstered his gun. He went over to the bushes, leaned, peered, straightened, looked back. He said:

'It's young Remy. I guess that explains things.' The others didn't figure the last sentence. He paused, scratching his head. Then he went on. 'You got him plumb in the brisket, Red. He's deader than a skunk. You've got some explaining to do.'

'I told you. . .'

'Yeh, you told me. But I don't buy it.' LaVere looked at his two boys. 'Get that body out of there and put it in the lean-to.'

They went forward. One of them said, 'There's a fine rifle here, chief.'

'Yes, I saw it. Well, bring it.' LaVere turned to Red again. 'Give me your gear. Bring your horse. I guess there should be another one around here. Have you seen it?'

'No.'

The body was moved by the two boys. A horse ambled out of the trees, halted, staring curiously.

'There's the hoss,' one of the boys said.

'For Pete's sake, bring him then.'

It was a strange, ominous cortège.

When Daggert woke up he wasn't sure where he was. Dawn was breaking. After lying on the hard ground Daggert felt edgy. And he ached in the most peculiar places. Loopy snored beside him.

Loopy had wanted to doss here instead of high-tailing it.

But how did Loopy figure he could get back at LaVere?

Why did Daggert let Loopy talk him into things?

Loopy, awake, staring up at Daggert as Daggert rose slowly.

'Let's get outa here,' Daggert said.

'I was figurin' on seeing the marshal,' Loopy said.

'That's Joe Pilgrim,' Daggert said. 'He'd chew our ears off. Anyway, you an' me have never dickered with the law an' I wouldn't like to chance it.' Daggert thought fast, or tried to. It wasn't easy. But then he said:

'Let's mosey out a-ways first. We'll think o' somep'n.'

The idea wasn't particularly bright but it was all Daggert could come up with. He was overjoyed when Loopy said, 'All right, we'll do that. But I ain't leavin' this territory yet.'

Their horses were far away, browsing. They mounted up. They stopped at a small stores on the edge of town, roused a drowsy keeper and got provisions from him, paying him good.

They were on the other side of the creek and past the willows when they saw the two riders coming towards them along the trail.

'Geez-us,' said Loopy. 'I didn't figure. . .' His words died away. It was obvious that they had been recognized. And the two riders were coming on faster.

They were Big Ade, and a sort of shambling-looking Pecos Dave, who seemed to have lost all caution, his eyes blazing with rage as he stared at the young man who, not so long ago, had taken a hand in torturing him.

Ade had been rough. But Ade was beside him now.

But the other one! He must be destroyed!

Ade was shouting as Dave spurred ahead of him. And Dave already had his gun in his hand. The first hint of the morning sun lit the frenetic scene in an eerie way.

Daggert and Loopy had been riding pretty close together but now they began to separate, both reaching for their guns.

Daggert shouted, 'What the hell. . . ?' But Pecos Dave was already shooting, and his first slug, though aimed at Loopy, took Daggert's hat off, made his horse buck.

Then Daggert was veering off at full speed into the morning sun.

Loopy fired. Dave swayed in the saddle but didn't fall off. Sweeping around him, Big Ade was shooting, and he was the best gunhand of all of them. He hit Loopy twice, once in the shoulder so that the boy spun half-around in the saddle. . . . And then another slug, the echoes rolling, plumb in the centre of Loopy's forehead, knocking him backwards off the horse as if he'd been propelled by an invisible wind.

Loopy's friend, Daggert, was almost out of sight.

Ade didn't go after him. Pecos Dave's mount had taken fright at all the shooting and was making for town as if all the devils of hell were at his heels, his rider swaying from side to side but holding on.

Loopy lay still, flat on his back now. His horse stood a little way off, looking curiously at the body.

Big Ade watched Pecos Dave go through the creek, still holding on. Dave would tell the tale in town, like aces he would!

'Oh, to hell with it,' Ade said aloud. He turned his horse about and rode back the way he'd come.

TWENTY-ONE

Marshal Joe Pilgrim, up early, was inspecting his new cell-block. The builders, working like slaves, and with help from some of the townsfolk, had finished the job in double-quick time. Three cells and a wide passage with a stout lockable door between that and the office. Stout log walls of a double thickness, the outer daubed with clay drying in the sun. The whole shebang virtually indestructible. Even a fire wouldn't be able to do the damage that had destroyed the previous set-up.

Soundproof too, Pilgrim reflected, not so much likelihood that Pug, dossing in the other place, would be awakened by a screaming drunk.

He went back into the office, then turned again, opening and shutting the communicating door, admiring its weight, and yet its smoothness also.

He heard hoofbeats outside. Somebody was in a hell of a hurry so early in the morning.

But the sound seemed to halt outside. Pilgrim went over to the front door and opened it.

He saw Pecos Dave dismount awkwardly from the horse and stagger on to the boardwalk, lopsided, one hand clutching his side. And that hand was dappled with blood.

Then, as Pilgrim moved out to help him, Dave fell.

He was trying to struggle to his feet as Pilgrim reached him, helped him get him through the door into the office and the old cushioned armchair which Pug often commandeered.

It appeared that Dave had either been stabbed or shot in the side. His face was damaged too: he'd certainly been in the wars. But he was trying to talk.

A sound behind him made Pilgrim turn. Pug came in.

'Fetch the doc,' Pilgrim said and the burly, moustached deputy nodded his head, unspeaking, and left swiftly.

Pilgrim gave Dave a clean cloth which the man held to his side, said he'd wait for the doc, didn't want anything else. It was obvious that he desperately wanted to talk, said something about 'he'd had enough'.

He told his garbled tale, ending with the revelation that he'd told LaVere that he'd be with him all the way, would even 'put paid' to Benny Grabe for him.

'I don't trust him, Joe. I just wanted to get away from there . . . after what they'd done to me . . . I just wanted to get outa there. . . . He wants you gone as well, Joe. He's a goddam greedy maniac. He wants the town – *and everything else. . . .*'

'It figures,' said Pilgrim gently.

The doc was here. Behind him was Deputy Jake who said, 'I saw Carrie. She says her an' her ma thought they heard shooting.'

'They did,' said Pilgrim. 'I want a posse. Get the usual boys, them who want to come along anyway.'

Jake went off. Doc said to his patient, 'Can you walk, son?'

Pecos Dave said, 'I ain't done so badly so far.'

'C'mon then. I'll fix you up, put you in the cot back in my place. You'll be all right.'

Dave looked at Pilgrim. 'Wisht I was comin' with you,' he said, sounding as if he meant it.

Pilgrim and Pug got their gear together.

The marshal was a bit of a connoisseur of guns. When he first came to Willow Flats he had a favourite Lightning Colt; but in a poker game, showing the locals he was no blue-nose, he'd lost this weapon, and a back-up Smith & Wesson to a gambler called Domino Harry who had drifted on to pastures new not long after, as his sort usually did.

Pilgrim had liked the man. He had heard later that Harry had killed a man who had accused him of cheating and was now in Yuma pen.

Now Pilgrim had a new Army Colt and a modified double-barrelled derringer (Harry would've loved that), together with his trusty Henry rifle, also modified somewhat, and a broad-bladed knife with a pressed-hide handle he'd had since he was little more than a sprig.

Jake returned, three more men with him, complete with horses and the warlike gear they'd figured they needed. The marshal only used a posse when he really felt he needed one. They looked at him, grim-faced, as he spelled things out quickly.

'It had to come like this eventually I reckon,' one said. Not many of the older, more sensible townspeople had taken to Brandon LaVere all that much.

On their way out they paused at the stable which the boy had just opened up, said he'd expected his boss to be here. But Red hadn't turned up yet. It was plain to see that Pilgrim was worried about his old friend. The boy insisted on riding a little way out with them, worried as he himself now was.

On the trail on the other side of the creek they saw the body in the dust, a horse standing near watching it as if on guard.

They gentled the cayuse, placed the limp blood-stained corpse of the younker whom none of them knew over its saddle.

The stable-boy said he'd take the horse to the

stable, the body to the undertaker. Maybe he had feared that the body might be that of Red. He seemed relieved to go back now. The rest of the purposeful bunch turned left off the trail, knowing where they were going.

Benny Grabe had awoken with a thumping head and a sore stomach, nothing unusual for him in recent times. His bedroom had a balcony outside which looked on to Main Street. Benny put on his pants and went out there. He saw the doc bringing Pecos Dave along and into the surgery. Dave seemed to be in a bad way, a walking wounded.

Benny went back to his wash-bowl and splashed his face and head with tepid water. He began to feel better. Last night he had seemed to hit an all-time low. Maybe something had happened to him during the night. He felt better, didn't even need a drink, he thought. He was curious about Pecos Dave, his old *segundo*, who'd been missing, gone over it seemed to what now Benny thought of as 'the other side'.

In his pants and moccasins, he went over to the surgery.

Dave was in bed but still talking, had a tale to tell his old boss who hadn't even stopped to put his wig on this morning.

Benny's eyes bugged – particularly at Dave's last words.

'He wanted you dead, *amigo*, wanted me to fix it.'

Benny went back to the Shotgun Place and put his wig on. He dressed properly, put his gunbelt on, got his shotgun, the one he'd had while on the stage lines, the one with which he'd once shot a road agent out of the saddle but hadn't killed him.

He was no gunfighter; but he'd been pretty good with the shotgun, he told himself.

Through the front window he saw the posse go by. After a while he followed them, far enough back to be out of their sight.

Big Ade had been out to look at the body in the lean-to.

He came back. 'Remy,' he said.

'I told you,' said LaVere. The two hardcase boys were there and Red the hostler was propped up in a chair, hands tied behind his back.

Ade said, 'Did you notice somep'n else?'

'What?' demanded LaVere. He was still more than peeved about what Ade had told him after coming back there; after not even touching the town; after seeing one man killed, another wounded and escaping, another gone for the high country.

'A wound in that body, in the side, a dog-bite, I reckon. Have you seen Gyppo?'

'Not lately.'

'I think he might have run into Remy and gone

for him. Maybe – maybe Remy shot him.'

Red spoke up. He wasn't gagged and had been mighty talkative, most of his language pretty colourful. 'The vet in town had a wounded dog in his surgery.'

'Gyppo was always a-roaming,' Big Ade said.

One of the boys was at the window. 'Folks comin',' he said. 'Looks like a posse.'

TWENTY-TWO

LaVere joined the boy at the window. 'Pilgrim,' he said, then seemed at a loss for more words, unusual for him.

Joe Pilgrim was down from his horse. He shouted, 'I want you, Brandon. Come out.'

LaVere didn't answer and Pilgrim tried again. 'Come out. Or I'll come in an' get you.'

Now LaVere had an answer. 'I've got your friend, Red, in here, Joe. If you move towards us I'm gonna have him shot.'

'That's not your style,' Pilgrim retorted, hoping he was right. Or was LaVere's Southern-gentleman act just an act after all, and he'd do anything – just anything – to get the upper hand?

He tried a ploy. A ploy that LaVere might fall for. His voice carried in the still air, in the sunshine of the bright, clear morning.

'You're the well-known gun-slick, Brandon. Try

154

me. You an' me, Brandon. Come out. Nobody else will interfere.' He was turning, looking at his men, all dismounted now. They all drew back a little.

LaVere was away from the window. Everybody was looking at him. But the only one who spoke was Red from his seat, upright in the stout wooden chair.

'You ain't got the guts.'

LaVere drew his gun, pointed it at the elderly, defiant-looking man. LaVere's eyes had gone a little odd. But he didn't shoot. He strode over to Red and struck out at him with the barrel of the heavy Colt. Red had been expecting something. He jerked his head to one side and the gun only scored a red line across his cheek. But he let his head fall on his breast. LaVere turned away from him and went over to the door. Then paused.

Suddenly everything was going to hell in a barrel.

He hadn't planned it this way. It was too quick, far too quick.

He had hardly started.

No reign of terror. No take-over of a town, a territory even.

Just Joe Pilgrim. Why? No, he didn't really have to ask himself why.

No grandstand play in the middle of Main Street. To show them all.

But he could show Joe.

He'd always wondered.

But nothing was for sure. . . .

He shouted, 'I'm coming out, Joe.'

'Come then!' Pilgrim's voice sounded almost friendly.

Another time maybe, LaVere thought. Another place and Pilgrim not wearing a badge. Two of a kind, LaVere thought. He opened the door and walked through it.

Pilgrim came forward, halted, his hands away from his sides.

LaVere had holstered his weapon. He walked like Pilgrim, arms swinging a little. Then, as if figuring the distance was just right, they both halted.

Neither of them fell into a crouch as some gunhawks did, that was not their way.

'Take me,' LaVere said, and his hand dipped, clawlike.

But Pilgrim was moving too. With a downward shrug of his right shoulder.

They were both right-handed men.

LaVere's gun was only at waist-level still, the muzzle beginning to tilt, aim, when the bullet from Pilgrim's iron bored into the man's shoulder, spinning him, propelling him to the ground, his gun flying from his hand.

He rolled, came up on to his knees, blood already dripping from his wound and colouring the dust with red blotches under the morning sun. His gun winked at him. But it was too far away.

'I didn't aim to kill you, Brandon,' Pilgrim said. 'Just to take you in.'

LaVere was down in the dust like a beaten dog.

He couldn't stand it!

He scrambled to his feet and turned; and *ran*. Joe didn't shoot him in the back. No! And he burst through the door and across the room and past the standing people, the man in the chair, the staring eyes; then he was in the hall, still running. And he went through the kitchen, blood streaming from his shoulder.

Suddenly, he stopped dead, realizing what he'd done.

The outer door was a little open. He reached behind, and with difficulty, blood streaming from him all the time, took his back-up gun from the back of his belt, wondering why he hadn't pulled that on Joe Pilgrim. . . .

Joe would've killed him for sure. He took a few more steps forward and opened the door.

Benny Grabe, unseen, had made a small detour and came in at the back of the house. And was standing next to the lean-to when LaVere came through the back door, a gun in one hand, his other hanging limply, blood dripping from his fingers and the sodden cloth above.

He stopped dead and exclaimed, 'Benny', his eyes wide, almost mad. He tilted the gun; but Benny said, 'Hallo, partner,' and he had the edge;

he pointed his shotgun and let off both barrels.

LaVere was hit as if by a terrific gust of wind coming suddenly off the prairie, and his heels kicked up as he went backwards through the door. His head hit the hard floor and he stretched out and lay still.

Big Ade, never the sort to argue with a posse bristling with armoury, lumbered through the hall, heard the shots. Then he hit the kitchen and stumbled over a body. He almost dropped the gun he still carried in his hand, careering forward as he fingered it, tried to raise it as the open door, sunlight streaming through, appeared before him; and he saw the figure standing beyond.

Benny hadn't had time to reload his shotgun, though he'd brought plenty of shells with him. But, quickly, he had drawn his hand gun.

'Drop it, Ade,' he barked. The big man let his weapon fall.

'Turn about an' march!'

Again Ade did as he was told, stepping over the shattered body of LaVere without mishap this time. Benny followed carefully and they went through the door, along the hall, through the communicating door as more shots rang out. But no bullets came their way. And Pilgrim was half-through the main door, a smoking Colt in one hand, his smaller back-up gun in the other. A young man sat in a corner with his hand clutching his shoulder, blood already seeping through his fingers. Another boy was against the wall by the window with his hands in the air, and between him and his wounded partner two guns lay on the floor.

In the middle of the room the elderly hostler called Red was seated tied to a chair.

Benny stepped aside from Big Ade. He holstered his handgun and, with the other hand, pushed the butt of his shotgun at the marshal, saying, 'I got LaVere, Joe. He's in the kitchen.'

Pilgrim had put his smaller gun in back of his belt again. He took the shotgun and said, 'All right, Benny.' Then, taken by some sort of surprise again, he turned once more to the door in the kitchen as Pug and Jake came through it, the latter saying, 'LaVere's in the kitchen. He's. . .'

'We know!' More men were coming through the front door, guns out, but soon pouched now. Steel flashed. Red's bonds were cut and he rose, massaging his wrists.

Pilgrim turned on Big Ade. 'I want you to point a finger or few for me, big feller.'

'Sure, Joe,' said Ade. 'But they'll be goin'. The rest of 'em. I'll see. I know. You'll see! Nothing around here for them now.'

'All right,' said Pilgrim.

Spryly, everybody was moving again. . . .